Poles Of Life

Farah Haseeb

Invincible Publishers

First published in India in 2017 by Invincible Publishers

ISBN: 978-93-86148-29-2

Invincible Publishers
F-55, Sushant Lok II, Hong Kong Bazar Lane Sector 57, Gurgaon-122003

Opposite Kasturba Ashram, Radaur Distt Yamuna Nagar, Haryana- 135133

Printed at : De Unique, New Delhi

Preface

A tale of 4 major pillars in the media of each region;

Politics the might, business the rule, bollywood a life style and cricket the religion.

Of INDIA u will get to witness the various shade;

That its hue is partially too bright and partially so fade.

Her too much blessings, turned for her a curse;

Like in too much of light, the vision goes blurred.

A tale with a glimpse of "white collar dirts" & its symbiotic association;

To achieve its benefit, they do stay in fake relation.

The wounded soul then left her world, and got transformed;

like a "phoenix", she rose back from her ashes in a new form.

After hardships, in true love her lost peace she found;

But was chosen by her destiny to have fame around.

Travel her journey of "poles of life", depth of destiny you will discover;

With this tale of spiritual reviaval, pain of souls will be recovered.

" This story is purely fictious and any resemblance to any alive or dead is just a co incidence."

Acknowledgment :-

Writing is something so pious to me its my passion and pleasure.

So first I want to thank ALMIGHTY!!! To bless me with this precious talent, to imagine and then to make my imagination do appear to this world with my words.

Today I am able to write so that I can touch your heart, this thought of sheer goodness was imbibed in me by my parents, so I really want to thanks my dear PARENTS who always did their best to give me everything at the best.

We can't grow higher if we aren't anchored to a worthy support, and to support me at the best in every walk of my life I want to THANK my two sisters Fatma Haseeb & Zainab Haseeb.

It's been always said, "The one who is appreciated, achieves more than what they try for". For this job I am thankful to my friends who always had encouraged me with their kind words and made me feel I really do write well. So thanks to Amna Rahman, Ambreen Fatima, Arshi Khan, Khadija, Firdaus Khan, Mezoon Badar, Shambhavi Gautam & Smriti Smita (names written alphabetically, all are my love)

A million thanks to all my teachers too to carve me well.

I am thankful to the awesome "Invincible publisher"; who was so nice and cooperative with me all time.

I really want to thank to all those, whoever had put me down for my passion of writing, because it's because their coarse words, that had polished the writer inside me to shine even more.

And last but not the least, I want to thank myself who never had given up in life ever.

"My heart does echo and mind does speak;
So silently in words, they do flow at its peak.
So when my silence and loneliness, do share intimacy;
Will make you fall in love, with my words like crazy......"

Dear Readers,

" This novel is entirely dedicated to you all, because I really believe that a good reader who senses the depth of each word is equally important as the one who pens it down".

So what do you think, too much of illuminations really do make you to twinkle like a glittery gem?

If you think so, then lets see the other side of the coin, where you will get to witness that, some time too much brightness makes our vision blurred and we start to see the world from that hazy veil.

With this journey of 'Her'; traversing, "The Poles of Life" and at the end you will experience the sense of spiritual revival.

Yes!!! She was the most awaited child of the nation, blessed with, "beauty of charm, power of the might and love of the hearts".

Her each move was an attention for the nation and each of her dream used to come true, before it was spoken in complete sentence. So now you can imagine how lucky she was.

Yet !!! In the depth of those immense blessings of love, luck, wealth, popularity and beauty; while growing up with days she felt a void in her life.

Slowly that void expanded and corroded her from so deep within that she went hollow from her soul.

So she forced herself to burn into ashes as a Phoenix and rose back from that ash, to face the world again, with a simple aim to achieve "the Satisfying Peace of heart"...

Contents:-

Chapter 1 - That day

Room no. 7 of Hospital Life Line at New Delhi, it was the worst evening of any autumn of my life, at 5.30 on 16th march. Me, Samar Asad was in my same cement coloured school shirt, which I had put on, on the last paper of my twelfth boards with my father Asad was in his favorite black old shirt soaked with the sweats of his nervousness.

At the moment we both were together but lost in the silence of pain; when the bright day was submerging with the dark night and so giving a hazy tint to sky. When the birds were roosting back to their nest.

My mother Ashika Asad was struggling with her few last remaining breathes; which were giving a siren that she is trying a lot to return back to normal state, but it was like slowly her pulse were getting hijacked by some unseen power.

Many machines that were attached to her, were unfortunately illuminating the colour of danger that is red, the pipes attached to her hands were pouring blood and saline inside her body.

There was a huge rush of media outside the door. Yet my brave mother in that phase of acute pain managed to say a few lines before camera.

But in that time of killing silence, she was continuously instructing me with her fingers towards the mirror and with the lovely eyes like of all mother, she too was trying to express love to them and then trying to say something to me from her pretty eyes, where I had always seen love for me.

It was hard for me to support my father in that hard time, yet I was trying to appear tough and fine for him, and he too was trying to support his young son , yet he was unable. In fact we both were broken like anything.

My mother on the bed with wounds, hasn't given up, her oxygen mask was removed on her demand, or perhaps the doctors understood it that she don't have much time. So they let her speak.

So she told dad and me that she love us a lot and will always be with us. Then to the cameras, to all the national journalists, she managed to speak with all her courage and some energy left inside.

"Please no conflict among any brothers or sisters over the issue of this bullet that had penetrated my skin and flesh, my end was destined this way, so it has to happen this way.

The reason of these bullets are always evils, but unfortunately they always do target the innocent, Ashika Asad is from all of you and ……."

I wish that may she could have got some more seconds so that she could have completed her sentence after the word " and"….,

But after that and.... she froze her eyes on me and my father, even at the ultimate end she tried and pointed towards the mirror again .

That moment the darks of night had completely taken over the brightness of the day; the birds were quiet after roosting back to their nests and it was silence in the darks ; when she left us alone in this big world forever.

Tears in my eyes were stagnant, may be my senseless mind and so my eyelids too forgot to drop them down and those tears were working like a magnifying glass; with which I was able to see the immense pain in the eyes of my dad which were stoned on the frozen eyes and cold body of my mother on that white bed inside that white four walls.

I collected some strength from the broken 18 years old Samar, who had grown a decade older in those few hours, and hugged my dad tightly and then I cried aloud.

Because I didn't have much power to keep that poison of pain for any more seconds inside me, but I got to my senses that my father was lost in his sad silence.

So I tightened the grip of my hug, so that I can hug his heart deep inside, within which the pain was hidden.

I was scared that my father who already had been in comma during my childhood, how would he cope up with this?

But its true, a father is always bigger than a son, so he put his palms on my cheeks and said, "Your mom was a great lady, had managed the life at her best, so God will welcome her at his place.

Then she was very tired, she was in pain since long and now the thresh hold of that pain was too much to bear, so she has gone to rest." Then wiping my tears he said, "let her rest in peace, she is always with us".

For the sake of my father I went quiet, that time we hardly bothered about this world, those media or anything. My mom needed her last farewell; So she was taken to our home town Banaras "the land of salvation".

It was telecasted on all channels that the famous writer and a social worker had died a few minutes back and the body of Ashika is mixed with the five essence of this universe and so is burned and the pious ashes of Mrs. Ashika Asad was submerged beneath this neutral soils of this earth, in our home courtyard .

Her pious ashes was buried in our home, because she said she wanted to be in that house forever. Many of our well wishers like the party members, mom's students, peoples from NGO and neighbors came to console us.

After her last farewell in our home, my father was busy seeing the news channels, on all of those channels it was all about my mom.

That how from "No one she became a Someone" her life journey is important for this world to know about. After watching those news my father came towards me with a plate of dinner and told me to have a little.

I was looking on him surprised, then he said; "We both have not eaten since a past couple of days. And your mom will never like it , she must be watching and getting angry over this. She would think that I didn't care about your health again and I promised her that you would eat on time. So please let me to keep up to my promise my son, I can only eat if you will take a bite."

Hearing this I put one bite in his mouth and one in mine like my mom used to do some times, and then i took the plate from his hands and kept it on the table and held his hands.

At this moment my father too couldn't manage to act strong, so he was broken deep and drained out his pain a bit with his drops of tears. Being practical I was happy that he is trying to ooze out that poison of silent pain.

After that dinner I made him sleep, I made him lie on the bed, switched off the lights and went out. Though I was knowing soon after I will go from his room, he will take out the pic of my mom and will talk to her. So to check, that he wasn't crying I stood behind the door, and heard him saying to my mom's pic, " Look Ashika, our Samar has grown up; to a nice and a responsible human being for which you have always desired and prayed for".

Hearing him, I wiped my tears and moved to my room Each corner everything and all the things were reminding me of my mom. If those toys were telling me about that innocent, lovely and crazy childhood ; when I was happy for no reason , then those books were telling the story of my adolescence when I used to avoid them yet had to deal the battle with them.

From each of those particles there, there was emitting the frequencies of my mom, and that frequency really had the aura of that pure and true love.

For some seconds I was lost, but soon I saw my reflection in the mirror and my sad face lost in sorrows, it made me to come to the real world ; where my mother was not around me.

Yet the magic of her motherhood and the blessings of her prayers, might had been supporting me. That is why I think, I was still able to breath in that phase of extreme pain.

Soon the reflection from that illuminated mirror, took me reverse to 24 hours; where my mom's last signal with her fingers was towards the mirror.

With this thought, my senses went in conscious

state again, what she wanted to speak? Why she was pointing toward the mirror? What was behind that?

When I was lost in all those webs of why and what; my mind after a long span of hours, managed to work and asked me to check out all the mirrors of our home, may be there must be some clue that my mom wanted to tell me in her last time.

I started from my dad's room to mine, to all the washrooms dressing table, wardrobe etc. but I couldn't get any clue. With last hope I entered in the room where my mom used to keep the idols of lord Rama.

In that small room also there was no mirror, I was depressed that I couldn't even get to know, that my mom was trying to say in the end.

With a pain of disappointment I took my steps back from the room. I was worried that in this world of countless mirror I will never get to know that what she wanted to tell me at her last moment?

I knew it so well, that if my mom had pointed towards the mirror then there must be some reason. Soon I was stepping out from the room; then my phone rang.

It was from the commissioner of capital, who said, "Soon the man who shot my mother will be arrested because the police was successful in tracing him. But to prevent the chaos it was kept away from media yet."

Hearing him, I felt a bit better; that soon I would be able to see that devil who shot out my angel like mom. I felt like killing that pig that did this sin for no reason.

If one part of me was boiling in anger, then other side was worried because I wanted to know what my mom was trying to tell me at the last? It must be something very important so she was continuously trying for it in the moment of her unbearable pain.

When I was just taking my last step out from that room, then above the door of the exit wall I saw a photo frame; which was a photo of my dad.

I was a bit surprised that in the worship room one of his picture is there among all pictures and idols of God.

Then in the glass of that photo frame, I was able to see the hazy tint of mirror image of lord Rama. Then I turned back and I saw just opposite to the door on the shelf, there was a big frame of lord Rama .

Whose image was being reflected in the picture frame of my dad. My feet automatically started moving towards that frame and in that frame of lord Rama, the shadow of my father picture frame I was able to see.

I had been a sort of 'gen y nihilist' means a confused next generation teenager who didn't believe in God too strongly, who had been to God only at the time of help. So I have never inspected that room so minutely ever.

I remember my parents were the most loving couple on this planet, my mom always used to say, " that my father isn't just her husband but a God, so she not just love him rather worshiped him".

My loving father used to say for my lovely mom, that my mom isn't just her wife rather she is his lady luck angel; so he doesn't see any happiness in his life beyond her".

That time my poor mind worked richly for the first time and had instructed me that, dad and lord both were worshiped by my mom as God, so they are mirror image of each other for her.

Word mirror again struck my mind, may be the

reason that why she was pointing towards the mirror must be around here, near to me. Towards which my mom was pointing.

I went closer to that frame of lord Rama and touched it, on it still there were the ashes of the effervescence stick, which my mom used 48hours ago when she prayed for the last time. Still I was feeling the smell of her around me in her unseen presence.

Then I dragged the frame towards me, so I felt something was there beneath it. I lifted it up, and then I saw a big dairy of white colour was there underneath, on which it was written "The poles of life".

In between its pages there were many dried lilies, I took it in my hand and put the frame of God back on its place and sat on the floor with that diary.

It had it's pen place in the last page, the date two days back from now, seeing it, I again felt my mom so near to me. I was feeling like just 48hours back she was here and in few hours she traveled far so away from me in some other universe.

Yet today from her each word in that diary, I was feeling her around again, her lilies fragrance was giving a sense of her unseen aura.

With this I thought to read it from the first page, I thanked God first time, from the bottom of my heart; that finally I would be able to know what my mom was trying to speak at the last?

Moment when I tuned the first page, I heard azaan and with that my father woke up as if it was his alarm. Just to show him that I was all right, I went back to my room and pretended as if beneath the blanket I am sleeping well. Because I don't want to make my father more worried.

Soon after the prayers, my father came to me to wake me up with the gentle blow on me of those sacred prayers, that he had during namaz. That moment I missed my mom again, who used to put tilak on my head after arti, the part of her prayer .

And I always used to tease her for the smaller tilak and bigger sweet as prasad Since long, my parents had been waking me up like that, so that his future IPS officer's son can start to prepare well for it and so with them, now it was my dream and aim too.

But this morning neither my mom was there nor my father was asking me to study, he just told me to wake up because he had to take me somewhere.

I was already awaken but I was acting like I was sleeping, so with a heavy voice I tried to act like that, but it's true parent always know us better than us. Because they is the one who has been knowing us since we were not knowing ourselves.

So he told me not to act much, because I don't know to act well. Hearing this, and that he knows that I am acting at once I got up.

Then he told me that he wanted me to go out in the garden.

I was looking on him surprisingly, then he said that he doesn't want me to go for a morning walk with him, but in the garden he wanted to plant lily; on the place where the ashes of my mom was buried. Because lily was the favorite fragrance of my mom and so she always used to have the perfume of lily."

My dad was already prepared with a small lily plant in his hand, I understood that he had been planting lily so that each day in his morning and evening walk; with the rise and the set of the sun he will be able to feel mom near to him with the scent of lily.

So with a smile full of love and respect, I looked towards my dad and held his hands and went out to plant it. Soon after we planted it, I was in a hurry to read those words of my mom. So I told my dad that I had to study.

I was back to my room and my father started his morning routine of walking like all days. I have grown up seeing him doing this every morning after his prayers.

I was touching that dairy with so many attached emotions of love and was missing my mom. I thought to call my father too, then I thought he will miss mom more after reading it, so I didn't.

Before opening it; I didn't know that my mom Ashika Asad had really traveled "The Poles of Life" and had seen it's extremes. So she wrote a novel on this and her personal diary too.

Her dairy was written just around a year back but the story started from around 39 years back.

Chapter 2 - I was lucky to be blessed

38 years 9 months back, the whole nation was waiting that who will be more than the luckiest and the most blessed child after the gestation of nine months. The family was not just the fusion of religions but there existed the fusion of the most powerful, elite, famous and prestigious fields of our country and they were politics means myth, business means the power, cricket means the religion and Bollywood means the lifestyle.

So each day before the birth, the baby bumps, diet chart, room design, shopping plan etc. were making headlines, meant inside the uterus someone was getting all those loads of media attention, for which one starts to dream at least after one and a half decade of their life.

And such a craze, such hype was natural because the pregnancy news of the heart throb of the nation's the famous film star, the owner of many awards for her best roles, Mrs. Ratika Gaur Singh.

If on one side it was making her fans depressed that for a long she would not be seen on the silver screen with her oomph moves, then at other side peoples were happy that the ultimate hot bombshell would soon enter in the race from the sexy diva to a yummy mummy.

So Mrs. Ratika was taking even a spoon according to her planned schedule by the best dietician.

Even some of the producers were angry at her unplanned pregnancy and then this news was a buzz in media by the extra concern of the paparazzi.

But the competitors of Ratika were damn happy that they will get a chance, because Mrs. Ratika Gaur wasn't just a celebrity in herself, rather she was the only daughter of the tycoon of the nation, Mr. Mahesh Gaur, and so her title Gaur was enough for her to gain an easy access to the world to cinema.

Where many actresses of her time had got entries after many struggles and compromises, but for her it was an easy ground, inspite of her countless tantrums; because her dad was enough to buy the makers of movies for making the only dream of her daughter come true.

Since Ratika had been the favorite child of her dad because when she was small her parents had split from their business and from each other too.

So like this, Ratika had been enjoying all the wealth, luxuries, media attention etc. since her childhood. So nothing was new for her at all, life had been like an easy bed of roses for her; that is why the entry and grip in Bollywood too.

Else she too would have to take along way of struggles like other actresses, either by small screen, or any title of beauty pageant and then to acquire the grip over the cut throat competition on screen she would have to be the girl friend of the most eligible, most dedicated and deadly handsome and a ruler hero. She would have to first attain the summit and after that it would have been easy for her to marry and earn another power title.

But Ratika didn't have to go through all those ways like other on the silver screen.

Miss. Ratika Gaur after becoming Mrs. Ratika Gaur Singh, wife of Mr. Vikram Singh who had added four moons to her. She was the daughter of the tycoon who was ruling the roost of silver screen and the wife of Vikram Singh was on the pinnacle of cricket ground.

A ground where not just matches were played, but the games are treated like battle, and victory was more precious than anything. A ground where the sweat of the players bring more wealth and fame than any other game player in the nation.

Though the way to this highly esteemed ground isn't too easy for everyone, but for Vikram Singh it wasn't even so tough because he was the only son of the ex. CM of the state and the head of the opposition party Mr. Dipesh Singh.

So one call of his father was enough to make the selectors committee of the nation to take his son in the team.

So it was quiet evident that the child of Mrs. Ratika Gaur Singh and Mr. Vikram Singh was famous through out the nation before his/ her birth.

People had started betting that the baby is going to be a boy or a girl, some corners had gossip that the perfect couple were shopping blue not pink so it will be a boy.

Even some said that because they were big people, they might know the sex of the baby prior to the birth.

It again made the headlines that 'shopping in blue confirms that sexy Ratika will soon be a yummie mummie of a smart son like her husband Mr. Vikram Singh'.

Even the opposition party of Dipesh Singh claimed that in their family sex determination is done, and this way the unborn baby was even brought into controversies before the birth, in the entire media of the nation.

Other wise for a normal person it is possible only in their adulthood, the 'blue shopping' had played a great role without any evidence and for some days had served a nice snacks with tea time gossips.

But all were proven wrong; when the birth of super lucky, extra blessed baby was pink. Means the baby was a girl, and so it spread a news of happiness, putting all rumors to be wrong and the nation welcomed the baby as a princess.

What will be the name of the princess? How is her mom after her birth? Which royal guest will be coming at the tinsel villa in the grand party of her birth? Media was catching and spicing up each of the news and was magnifying them all so well.

Finally after a week of that much awaited birth the day of that royal dazzling party arrived, if the gate of tinsel villa was invisible under the rows of Mercedes, Rolls Royce etc. then inside that majestic bungalow the heaven like decoration was illuminated more with the twinkles emitted from the diamond jewelries of the guest.

In that moment of regalia, finally after many searches for the name of the princess, the name was announced as ISHIKA GAUR SINGH.

Ishika was the name of the newly arrived pink life and her powerful surnames Gaur and Sigh were enough to show the strength, wealth, respect and popularity associated with her.

And this way Ishika, soon after her birth was more popular than Miss India, and in the age of seven days she was shot for the advertisement of Pampers and Johnson's like baby product, so the baby was the brand ambassador of two big names at the age where a child just knows to sleep and cry.

Ishika was fair, light eyed and lovely like her mom. She had a tall slim and a sporty physique of her dad. It was all explored by the world in a mere duration of 7days in which all babies look all most the same.

Though that was not a time of digital cameras, mobiles and Facebook yet Ishika's pictures were everywhere in all poses either she was eating, sleeping, smiling, playing, bathing, drinking, crying etc.

If on one side her looks were in gossips, then at other side her powerful gene that she inherited from all the powerful grounds were in discussion of what Ishika will become in the future?

A tycoon? A heroine? A sports person? Or will go in politics? In the beam balance the quantity of blessings for her and the prediction for her future both were around to be equal & a lot.

Chapter 3 - World of lovely dreams...

I, Ishika Gaur Singh, was growing up. I didn't know but it was all becoming news that when I first spoke the words maa paa, when I learned to walk, when my first deciduous tooth came.

And in my case, it was rare that my maxillary central incisors, meaning the upper front tooth came first rather in normal cases lower front appears prior to the upper, even what I like? When I sleep? All was in the news and shows. I was the brand ambassador of few more products like health drinks for under 3 babies etc.

If at one side my popularity was going up and I was unaware of it, on other side my mom was aware that her improper vital physical statistics her washboard belly etc. were in need of some tummy tucks.

For that duration Ratika wasn't ruling the roost of item numbers and movies but was showing it well to the world that she is happy to be a mother.

She was too busy doing many new advertisement like those of health drinks during pregnancy, pregnancy test kits etc. Later was popularizing her gym where she used to do yoga and aerobics during the time of her pregnancy with all the elite and polished ladies like her.

She used to discuss in the interviews about her diets which was planned to benefit both the child and the mother, and now she was giving tips how to be a yummie mummie so that they still have the same charm on their husbands.

She used to narrate the world on how to nurture your baby well so that the baby has a balanced physical and mental growth and at the same time how to mold her to become a good human being...

Amazingly it was all far from the reality, my health and growth was looked by a well trained professionally qualified nanny and thanks to God I was growing well under the hands of my grandmother Eliza Singh.

It's said that when a child grows up they first recognize their mom and feel attached to her the most, but I was highly attached to my granny and recognized her more than my parents.

But this world was believing and listening to all the motherhood tips and advice of Mrs. Ratika as if she was the first mom of this world to give birth to her baby and to bring her so well.

The fact was she was so busy in the gym shedding her extra flab for the next movies that were pending since long because of the 'un planned me'.

So gym, parlor, shootings, parties and interviews used to keep her so hooked up, that the best my mom could do the only thingfor her famous baby was to kiss her . if I woke late in the night when she used to return, and that kiss was a loud muuaaah, with least affection and all that came out from her mouth was I love you my baby.

And my dad was on higher on success, in the most majestic ground of cricket he was the king meaning, he was the captain of Indian cricket team.

He always used to say I was lucky for him. My

arrival had given him more success but the session of crickets, practice, interviews, and advertisements of various brands used to keep him all time out of home.

So when he used to come back home, he always showered me with all the prettiest imported dolls, dresses and chocolates and used to take me for drives, to have my favorite ice-cream together.

But I had always hated that my sweetest moment that I used to treasure with my dad after a long used to be snatched by media and cameras and questions.

But I grew up learning myself, that we are the celebrity class so each of our move is important to be caught and displayed by media among the mass.

It was all about my mom and dad I understood till now. So in my views mom is one who give birth to her baby, at night she kisses her and says I love you, take her to parties, shopping and interviews.

And dad is the one who when comes home bring a lot of gifts and takes for for ice creams.

I was 4 years old when I started going to school, and right from my school bag, stationaries and lunch box were all in discussion; its color and brands all were drawing interest.

More brands for advertisements had signed me, my likes dislikes, my favorite color, my most watched cartoon all were more read than the important issues of the nation.

May be in our country common man loves the celebrity so much that in their happiness they forget their grieves and this is what was happening with Ishika's life too.

My school was bigger than the all other schools of the nation where almost all kids came from big homes in shiny cars. Yet I was the most focused one. I was happy that in my lower kindergarten I was signing autographs merely by writing my name in capital letter.

Now at four years of age I was happy to see myself on television in various advertisements and shows, my pictures from childhood till now.

I was a fair light eyed small girl in her pink and blue combination school uniform with two pony tails having sweet clips, a load of Mickey mouse shaped school bag on the back and a flower shaped water bottle around my neck. Now I was happier to see and recognize myself as a pretty child in the newspapers and on TV.

Because my friends were not there and not even they used to look like Cinderella in the fancy dress show like me so I was slowly developing a sense of pride in me, without knowing what actually being proud is, I started feeling it.

In that small age I understood that I was different from my friends that time. I didn't know the word 'superior' but I used to feel so over my friends. I thought I was so nice that is why teachers were so polite and loving to me even when I was caught talking or sleeping in the classroom.

I also didn't know that I was luckiest to be blessed so much that all of them wanted to have a picture with my mom and dad and wanted to see them and to meet them in the parents teacher meet.

But many parents teachers meet came and went and from lower kg, I went to standard 7th. I was almost in the most beautiful days of my life and that was my teen age in all these years my height was increasing with my age. Even my hair had grown longer.

But in these years one thing that was common

was, in all my parents teacher meet I used to go with my granny, yeah during my birthdays my parents managed to come to my school to invite all for its grand celebration at my tinsel villa.

Now after looking into the mirror, I was able to sense how beautiful I was, looking on my status I understood I was superior. It all just not made me arrogant but also boosted up me with attitudes and tantrums. I knew it was the reason all girls pretended to be my friend but none of them were actually my close and dear friend.

I used to take it lightly assuming that they all were jealous of me. Now I was enjoying being interviewed, was happy being in limelight of media and loved to endorse more brands.

I never knew how at the ultra last moment of my birthday my mom and dad managed the time at the exact moment when I had to cut the cake before many cameras. My parents used to give me big gifts and kisses as if they are always with me, in my birthdays all the guests who had entry pass were with the best of their gift, which was checked before being handled to me for the sake of safety purpose.

In that ravishing party all were in the best of the bests they could because that party had fusion of all the royal pillars of the nation film, sports, politics and business under the shade of media.

And our costumes were designed by the biggest designer, interiors were from the most demanded decorator and the return gift were really the chosen one which was enough to describe our majesty.

All the cakes, food and stuffs were from the biggest brands were on the best display of my luxury in the party and in the headlines.

It was all making me happy but the thing that actually used to satisfy me was the pure love of my granny that was with me since I was born. She used to take me to church in the morning when there was no one and used to give me simple gifts.

I never knew how that arrogant girl loved those simple gifts like doll , story books etc. the most. Among all other precious gifts, my parents also use to take me for prayers at gurudwara and temple but not for the God there, rather for the camera around us.

Yes I was enjoying camera in those sacred place but wasn't feeling that peace which I used to feel when I was with my granny, why it was all so I wasn't knowing may be I was young to understand it all and couldn't even ever got the time to talk and ask my parents how I felt.

My parents managed to be at my school in some shows and that also never ever together, just for a fraction of minute and for that small duration many arrangements were made, and all were crazy to have a picture with either my mom or my dad, whoever attended.

If at one side I was sad that both of my parents don't come together then at other side I was happy thinking that how important figures my parents were, and so used to console myself saying happily that even if just one of them came, so much of arrangements had to be made. If both of them came, then what would have happened.

This way my age, my class, my popularity, my attitude and tantrums and yes with my glowing beauty was rising up the ladder.

I was born, brought and taught that all these media attention is important to us, and I too started liking it. My life was more people's than for mine and I loved it to be discussed.

All the time I was in demands. Now from the kitty party to award party of mom and from the cricket matches to election campaign of my grand father, I was always seen on television and newspapers and that newly growing up teenager was loving that twinkling phase of life. For me it was a normal life, may be because I didn't struggle for it so I didn't know it's worth But one day I realized that my life also has some stains of query associated, no matter how small they appeared to me, but with my growing age I started understanding it.

Like I used to hear people using sentences like, 'now Ratika is a cold item for hot item numbers, her lovely bud will prove to be much hotter than her on stage and set fire with her tighter curves'.

After coming back home, I went to my mom to discuss about it, and in her red saree she was looking awesome. I complimented her, and then told her about all theses comments, and my mom was in hurry and getting late to put on paints on her face and body for the party.

So she just told me that in life we come across variety of people with their own school of thoughts and it's impossible to deal with all of them, so I should just stay chill over this.

The cool and carefree words of my mom made me relax for that moment but deep in my heart those sentences were still echoing but reasons and solutions for that wasn't with that small and innocent me.

With the tide of time I had completed my

schooling along with many other things like painting, singing, dancing, yoga, piano, horse riding, and swimming courses one after other; because after school I was indulged in all these to be trained as jack of all fields or to be much praised in media that the super girl of super family is trained and superb in all fields by the costly teachers.

But the fact was, my parents never had much time for me.

So I was indulged being busy and enjoying those well scheduled life which was always appreciated in media, I was also happy for these at that time or this was the definition of happiness I had learnt so far.

And slowly it came my last parents-teachers meet of my school life and again I was with my granny like the past decade and four years, over the absence of my parents none could dare to ask me directly not even the principal.

But one of my friend of my childhood came to me at the time when we were hugging each other for the last time most probably, questioned me that I never let her to meet my mom and dad, at this I was speechless.

My granny changed the topic and blessed her all the best, and with my granny came home but on the way I had been to church with her, and I was doing this since my childhood.

I never knew why with her in church far from the camera, those attention and hyped tantrums and make ups I used to feel free, happy and satisfied like never before; from the depth of my heart.

When I returned with my report card, I was happy to see my dad at home and he congratulated me for completing my school and said he was proud of me,

I don't know why he was proud?

I didn't top the exam ever, and with the face of national topper I was also in newspaper just for passing up the exam.

That time I felt I have never worked hard yet I was being appreciated and got to know it wasn't my identity. It was all because of my family. That day I took the first decision of my life and told my dad that I didn't want to go to foreign for my college, but want to do something and make out my own image.

At this my dad asked what I wanted to do. So I told him that God has blessed Ishika with some talent too, and that's the talent of being able to sing songs with melody on the note of piano that she learnt to play

Hearing this my dad was silent and my mom entered from the door to my room with a smile and surprisingly she managed to come early, I thought she was there for me but she told her shoot was cancelled because of injury to the hero so she is there.

But at that moment she supported me and asked my dad to let me do what I want because now I am a big 17years old girl. At this my dad smiled and said he wanted to see me as the singing sensation.

I smiled nodded yes and hugged my dad, and hugging him I said that why in her complete school life her parents never had been for the parents teacher meet like the parents of all other students at her school???

At this my father looked at me then he was quiet and was looking at mom so that she might be able to answer.

At this my mom said being cool like everytime, that the parents of other students are not big celebrities like my parents so they have time. They didn't work round the clock so that they could give all the jewels to their daughter like I am having.

At this I managed to smile and said yes!!! And so all my friends don't change their Mercedes like me after few months, at this my dad came to me and said that's the reason my child.

I was knowing the reason, yet I managed to say yes to my dad, rather I too was knowing that all these aren't to give comforts to me, rather its all the part of their life style which they can't afford to alter for the small thing like parents teacher meet of their daughter.

I learnt to Ignore all those annoying aspects and was enjoying all the brighter part, I was working hard, my mom had already managed for the best lyrics on whose words of beautiful meaning I can sing a song of lovely melody.

Apart from this, a great music band, popular for its rap note was there to play music for my debut album "passion", my makeup artist my dress designer all were ready News was, in the air that soon my "passion" is going to be launched and it was like a buzz in the air again, and so it was predicted to be a mega hit before its release.

Because if I was working hard round the clock, then the mighty grounds of politics, business, Bollywood and cricket around me all were also devoting for it under the shade of media.

Yes!!! In all these, the best that was happening with me was that I got a good friend Vicky, the rrap musician, who was giving me a lot of time after my practice, we used to go for drives, to discs, to gym, in parties, to restaurants and last but not the least on telephone.

If "passion", my music was already my passion

then Vicky was my new passion. If he wasn't with me, then he was in my thought when I was awake and when I was sleeping, he was in my dreams.

I was lucky to enjoy all phases of my life at its best, yet this was the sweetest phase of my life. But one day my grand paa advised me that what I am doing is normal for the child of my age but all shouldn't come to camera before public, else his votes will be hampered because Vicky was from the group of his anti party. He suggested me to have a private friendship only till I wanted, but that time I was in my own dream world so ignored those serious words of my grand paa.

Finally came the day when my debut album was launched. Again it a scintillating party was thrown like all times, in which all the famous and big names from films, sports, politics and business world were there.

Though I was used to be at such parties, but this time it was special infact more than special for me, I had double reason to be happy and to go on cloud nine. One reason was the success of my " passion" and other was Vicky.

For whom I was feeling love I think, I wasn't knowing yet what love was but whatever I read so far about it in novels, all those symptoms were happening with me. I was happiest to see myself this time on news, for the work of my debut album Passion for which I really had worked hard.

It was on the headlines, 'born star has finally become the star', in other channel its said, 'the nation's youngest music sensation the passion star Ishika is the best'.

In parties to sign the real autograph for the first time I was on seventh sky, now I realized why my parents are addicted of this lifestyle.

I was interviewed, awarded, now I was signed up for many more new brands and even I was signed for my first movie of the biggest banner, but I was ignoring all these because Vicky was more than any gem to me now.

He meant more than world to me. I was waiting for his proposal despite of being so busy, and in so much demand. I was pretending in front of him that I was fine but the fact was that I was dying internally every moment to hear for the proposal from him without knowing if he loved me or not???

It was my first show abroad; in Hong Kong Vicky was also there with his band. The show was a real hit. The passion in his music, the charm of my sounds and my moves and turns, all those swirls over the notes made the audience completely go spellbound as if they were committed to shout in my appreciation; had given me an energy to go on with my passion.

After the show of passion, it was becoming tough for me to hold onto my own passion, and so I decided to tell him what I felt for him; but I didn't have that courage, so I took a few pegs and I entered in his room.

He was going to sleep and so he was changing, at once at late night seeing me there in my black short frock which I was wearing in my show and was appeared damn sexy, his eyes were wide open and jaws were dropped. I smiled seeing him and went closer to him and closed my eyes. May be vodka for the first time worked straight on me.

And I said him "So, Mr. Vicky a famous rap musician 8 years older than me, but still, so silly don't know that how much I love you".

Hearing this, he was silent and with a smile. I kept looking deep in his eyes and then he came so closer to me. I could feel his warm breath on me and then he kissed me deep.

The intensity of his kiss on my lips was enough for me to know that he too loved me madly.

Lost in his strong arms, his tight hugs, feeling each of his breath in the silence and his scent was deep inside my breath. I too was kissing him like it was the only true and the most precious thing that existed in my life and for which I am alive.

Not just my body, but my heart, my mind and my soul was loving him, and I was submitted to him with all my love, trust and concern and we made love.

I wasn't in my control, I was trying a lot to stop but the love in him didn't let me. Because that moment if I had controlled those emotions, then more than me it would have hurt him and to hurt him was like a sin to me, so to please him I was ready to commit a sin before God.

It was for the first time for me, after it I was a bit nervous but his love silently gave the courage to me, I made it with all my true devotion. The devotion with which pray and so thinking about this, I was normal, in morning he woke me with kisses and smile and asked me to leave before we become the prey of false media and paparazzi interpretation.

I hugged him tight and took my way back to my home.

In the streets of my own town, the city of dreams that is Mumbai, I was happy like anything to see my big posters as the star, but more than this, the thing that was pleasing me was the feeling deep inside me, the feeling of love for my first love Vicky.

Soon after reaching home, I planned to go to church with granny to thank God for giving me everything so perfect in life.

But while planning this I didn't know that sometime we don't plan life, rather, life plans for us and sometime its plans are unexpected to be welcomed.

And the same thing happened to me, as I got home, my only true friend to whom I was most nearest my granny was very ill, hearing this I was shattered. Soon I rushed to her room, which was looking like a hospital, two nurses and a doctor were there to take care for her. Grand pa was calling from Delhi to get her review but couldn't come because of his schedule.

Mom was abroad for shoot and dad was in Kolkata for matches. My sweet granny was well cared under the hands of strangers. Even among those nurses, doctors and servants she was appearing so lonely. But soon I went to her and touched her hands, she looked at me with that same smile of real affection, but because of her weakness she couldn't managed to speak to me.

Chapter 4 - The own plans of destiny...

Since past eighteen years I was really happy to be the luckiest girl, I don't remember last time when I was sad, may be I wasn't sad ever, some times I was annoyed, angry, lonely and irritated, but I had many reasons to be happy so this feeling of sadness was a stranger to me.

But at this moment of seeing my grand mom, I came to know sadness for the first time, I had read about these sad feelings in novels, had seen in movies and many times, I saw my mom acting sad in movies, yet I never had experienced it. But now I thought I was a big girl, of eighteen years have right to vote so should I must have the art to console this passion star inside me , thinking this I said to myself that all big doctors are caring for my granny and now soon she will be well and fine.

My live concert was coming next month for which advance bookings had started in my home town Mumbai, so I should be happy for this and then the biggest reason to be happy was that my love was with. For this I should smile.

Thinking about Vicky again I forgot all my pain, and since he was out of country, looking at his picture and feeling him near to me was the only option left for me.

To share about my love, I went to my best friend, my granny. Seeing her awaken I was happy, I went and sat near to her and said, "my granny, your daughter want to share something and that secret is that your little best friend is in love!".

She kept her wrinkled yet soft hands on my cheecks and squeezed it with smile and love and said the glow of my face was telling her better about this.

That day granny, told me that now I was a big 18 years old girl so she too wanted to share something with me, and she said she was an orphan. Her childhood and early teens were spend in a convent where she used to live with sisters and thought that she would also become one like them.

But that time she wasn't knowing that like and an angel, Jesus would send my grand paa in her life, who will love her like anything and to get her, he would go beyond all rules and will face everything, and granny told that her love had given him that power to face the world and his courage made her love him so much that she was ready to leave her world to hold his hand forever and since then till now they loved each other more than anything and above everything.

Narrating her story, she said if love was true it was everything to be more than happy, and unfortunately if it was not, then what disaster it brings in our life, we cant ever imagine.

Hearing her, I kissed her hands and said that love of ours is also so true, and I said her with a smile that after decades Ishika too will be narrating the story of her love to her young grand daughter, at this granny smiled and I was happy to saw her fine.

Talking and smiling with granny when I slept so

peacefully with her I didn't remember. Early morning I woke up by some sound of someone screaming, I thought that I recognized this voice, soon I understood, its mom and I was surprised that why is she shouting so early in the morning?

Her shoot got cancelled, I thought, that would be why she was back so early, to know it all I started walking to her room silently so that granny wouldn't wake up.

My house was big like a school campus so in few minutes I reached to her room there I saw mom was with her dad and a lady, and she was in acute anger, seeing me she went silent, and I too slowed down my steps and went to her to know what had happened.

My face had a big question mark and for the first time my mom was may be able to read my silent question and so had answered; may be this time it was for her own concern, so she managed to explain.

She said in explosive angers that the producers had just called her for a guest appearance role, and the reason that my mom explained to me for this was indifferent to my assumption.

As I thought that now many young actresses were there so my mom didn't get role, but she told that dad's shares are going down in the market these days and so he is not able to finance the producer and not even influential enough to turn the black money to white of the producers with their over seas collection, so the producers had done this to her.

The famous Ratika wasn't able to tolerate this humiliation before the media so she was angry like crazy.

Then at once that lady, a stranger to me came

towards me, looking eight to ten years older than my mother or maybe more I don't know.

Like the way my mom who also looks as if she is just five to seven years older than me with the help of her scheduled diet, gym and parlor but we all know mom can't be just five to seven years older.

That sexy lady in her coat pant and specs with golden hairs asked my mom in a foreigner ascent, "Rati is she your daughter?" And my mom nodded yes! simply without any delight to introduce her star daughter.

Because that time she was sad to be humiliated and that was more than anything for her. That lady came to me and said I was just like my mom, but I denied and said I am combination of all the family members from both maternal and paternal side.

At this that lady said then I must resemble her too, I was surprisingly thinking how I can resemble her? But in a moment she cleared my confusion. And hearing her I was shocked because she was mother of my mom, but technically she was looking a few years older than my mom and my mom used to look like my elder sister, not just in reel life but in real life too, truly! Wealth makes you a sexy and young grand mother.

After seeing my new granny, I just realized that I had an other relative too but she could hardly able to touch my heart.

Because when my mom was small, she left her and so my mom was never able to know what a mother is, and may be that's why I too couldn't feel it in an absolute sense.

Then they both I mean my nanoo and her ex wife took an exit from my mom room because they were getting late may be for some meeting as usual, soon after that my mom explained to me everything.

She wanted to share that moment actually with someone to lighten up her mood and so I gave my ears to her. She told that these days some foreign investments of nanoo are under consideration of income tax departments and so his money is not able to change from black to white, I never knew how money could have change like that.

Because I was actually a poor student of economics, then my mom explained that my nanoo has his major notes in black and so the investors are loosing hope with him. His shares are going down in the market, and so he is not having that hold in the market and thus all those producers who couldn't dare to speak a word to my mom because of her powerful father, are today giving small roles to my mom.

I wanted to tell my mom that soon everything will be fine, but my mom didn't give me any chance and with this, my mom got up and said she needs a massage and a steam bath to freshen and so she is leaving.

At that moment I too wanted to let her know that her daughter has proved to be a star at her first show and she is in love too, but without noticing me she went straight towards the door.

Then she stopped I thought she must have forgot something, but she smiled looking at me and said that her pa told her that he saw the newspaper that I dazzled at my show.

I wasn't sure if I should be happy that the famous actress, Mrs. Ratika Gaur Singh noticed me, or I should be sad that my mom noticed me even less than a stranger, these all made me still; without any reaction, she left from there but I was still there .

Suddenly I was happy to see that my weak granny was able to walk and came to me and asked me to switch on the tv because today my father was playing a match.

If that was my hot and sizzling mom who left me unheard and went to be freshen up then this was also the mom who took the pain in her weakest state to get up just to see her son playing and that also even on television.

At that time I thought that my granny was an orphan she too never knew who a mother is. Yet her motherhood is so perfect, then why has this world has sucked up motherhood of my mom who wasn't even an orphan?

I switched on the TV, and expected to see dad batting on ground, it was like all day happiness for me, but for my granny that happiness was always glazed as the new one, no matter her son , used to talk to her hardly, a very few sentences in the whole month.

India won the toss and the public in the stadium was cheering! That insane crowd was enough to state why cricket was worshiped like a religion, how the sentiments were attached to it and hence, why it was the wealthiest game in our country than any other sport.

My dad was an opener. My granny and I were excited to see him, and it was happening since my childhood that just granny and I used to enjoy dad's matches and mom's movies together. I don't remember last time when we all were together without media.

But this time again, I witnessed an unexpected experience of destiny. Dad was out on the first ball, I was sad but in the eyes of granny there were tears, and like us the expression of grief was there on the face of the viewers too. It was enough to prove how much the public loved the celebrity.

Seeing dad out, granny was sad and said she wanted to sleep so I turned the television off.

I too got up to eat something because since I was back from Hong Kong I was getting surprises after surprises from life which had deactivated my hunger.

Soon telephone rang and I understood it was grand paa's, because he only calls on land line to talk to granny, so I received and told him that she is sleeping.

At this he asked if we watched TV. I told him we did and were really upset to see dad got out in his first ball itself. Then he said that I should go and switch on the news channel. It had some things bad about dad, on hearing this I did as he instructed me seriously he told not to interact media until he reaches there.

Since birth, I had always seen media appreciating my dad, but today what I saw had shaken the ground off my feet. it was my dad picture on the screen, beside him it was written, 'the real face of Mr. Vikram Singh' and in a hazy video there was the rest room where players change and rest before the game .

There I saw my dad was with a slim and fair girl of my age in her ultra short pieces of dress and I could just see her half face where here small closed eyes, was visible. Rest was covered with the side face of my dad and her hairs.

And media was saying that was the real face of my star dad, it's the energy that Mr. Vikram took before his game and so he was out on the first ball.

It was hard for me to trust and to be calm and so I switched it off, soon mom and grand paa both reached home like they travelled on rocket in an emergency. My mom did not say a word over this. I don't know how she could be so composed to see all this.

Grand paa just asked us to say to all that it's a conspiracy. Some one tried to make a honey trap for my dad by mixing some sedative in his drink to black mail him.

Soon media was there in clusters outside our tinsel villa and about all those honey trap and conspiracy by the anti party. grandpa explained to all and said soon he will set an investigation department to find out who was behind all this.

I prayed it must be true what grand paa said, but the picture was saying everything, that time I understood why politicians were called so talented. I was they know the art to handle even the worst situations very easily well.

My grand paa too knew that art too so well. Perhaps that was why he was ruling the roost of politics since the past decade. That day India won the match, the victory gave some relief from the anger of the public.

Yet on the streets, there started protest against my dad. Soon I heard grand paa was shouting on the phone and he was saying to my dad, "You idiot! Couldn't you control your manhood for some moments? How can you be so ignorant about the camera??? It could all be done at a safe place in a safe time but now at the time of election how will I manage it all?"

Hearing grand paa and his lessons to dad it was clear to me that that video wasn't fake, and seeing mom normal, I got a reason to wonder if is the relation ship of my parents was fake and is meant just for the media and social party that they are such a devoted and a loving couple?

I was in doubts about my existence, broken deep

inside. Soon my phone rang and it was Vicky. Seeing his name I got a reason to smile, because I knew his love is deep and true for me, and he said me "Jaan, I am back and missing you a lot, so I want you this evening. Be there" I too wanted him near me and his arms to support me and his shoulders on which I can rest and forget all my pains, and so I told him that I would be there my love.

Avoiding all the issues, in his favourite colour black in a sexy black gown, I went to meet him. Walking to his way I was so happy that all worries were like oozing out and I was sure that after sharing it all with him I will get some energy to be alive.

So I lied at home that I am going for practice and so I would be late, and except granny all were knowing that I was going for practice or may be rest all were hardly interested to know that where I was going.

I entered his banglow guards greeted me and soon I went inside he was there sitting on sofa, seeing me he came quickly to me and without giving me any minute he hugged me tight and said he missed me, and I said me too my love.

He made me free from his arms and was looking at me deep. Then I opened my lips to speak something but he locked my lips with his and soon we were lost in love, after that passion, it was too late and he said I should be back to home, but I wanted to shtay with him but he said next time.

It was really late so I agreed and got back, at home. There things were tensed all were quiet so none noticed that from where I am coming so late, it was my parents there with their own parents, soon I heard grand paa was calling me to be with them.

I went to them, in the big hall my big and influential family was there, my parents with their own parents.

And then nanoo said that now my album was a mega hit, I could go to foreign to get a degree on music , if I want to give more flavor to my music and for this he had arranged everything. He handed me a file in which there were all he details of the universities in Europe and tickets for the next month and an ATM card, the second oxygen for this planet to survive anywhere.

My nanoo's thought was that only foreign degrees and collaborations can really make you big in real sense, and he might have been true in his views, then mom said after my up coming live show in Mumbai if I would like I can may leave for there, all arrangements were made for this.

But in all this my dad was silent and was avoiding eye contact with me. May be he was ashamed or something, but I never know how my mom was so okay to see her husband in the arms of some other girls.

Then mom said in my show I have to meet someone, and I asked who. At this my nanoo said I had to meet Siddharh Jain, his dad was opening a big university at our state for medical, engineering, MBA, nursing, pharma, CA, agriculture from the bachelor to the research level, and not just university many charitable hospitals, NGOs, rehabs etc.

At this I smiled and asked if they wanted me to be their ambassador. Well !!!... it wasn't a big deal....

I will be their ambassador, then my grand paa told that dad was trapped in this conspiracy, mom had lesser time in Bollywood and his party isn't able to do the big rallies and not even able to take media in its stride;

because its image is going down under the hands of anti party on the name of secularism.

So to raise back again he needs a huge sum and since a long nanoo was giving money to him and in turn grand paa political power was helping nanoo notes to stay white.

But now a days nanoo note were pigmented by melanin to black colour so heavily and he was in need a huge amount of fairness cream to turn it white means a huge might of political power and big shares

But those share holders were not interested to invest or to do anything for nanoo because his image was tarnished I don't know in all notes. our father of nation "mahatmaGandhi" ; is same so how notes can be black or white?

So in that conversation with grandpa, the only thing I understood was that our family was running on the wheels of politics, business, cricket and Bollywood was coming to a halt.

Hearing all this, I asked only one word. "So?".

At this dadoo said joining hands with Siddharth can help us; nanoo will become his business partner and he will fund for charities to keep his money white, he has his own co operative bank too, where inlet of black money ejects the whiter one.

So with a good image he will be able to attract big investors and share holders and money will attract money and then he will be able to help grand paa with that huge sum to advertise his party at the best and when his party will gain the position, then power will attract more money and with the synergistic effect of power and money mom movies and dad cricket will again be accelerated and then again money, power and fame will attract everything like ever.

I smiled to hear the big plan and asked, "How a singer as young as can help them?"

At this my mom answered and what she explained was totally unexpected, she said Siddharth was young, smart and rich and so I had to attract him towards me so that he could marry me and then their master plan could work. Hearing mom, I was on the top of my anger and refused, at this she asked why? Siddharth was a dream of all girls?

So I explained for this plan to buy our success I cant trap anyone, at this mom said its nothing like to trap, then I replied her straight that I cant do it because I am already in love with someone.

At this my mom smiled, and said love was nothing, I was a kid so I was saying all this. Life is all about being practical. At this I couldn't control and my hidden anger, which was silent for a long was exploded out that moment.

I said, "Yes! Life is all about being practical, we should become so much practical that we should learn to live even when our husband is wrapped around someone else's arm.

We should be so practical that we should separate our nation on the name of religion to be powerful, like grand paa's party which does profit in the name of religion causing vote polarization, but still the poor is struggling for a one time meal. That is why our country is. "Poor India of few Super Rich Indian"

"We should be so practical that we should hide our black money to be saved from taxes in the bank and at the end we should be so practical that if nothing works out, we should ask our daughters to sell her self to some stranger so that all the false shine and glaze can carry on, actually you all, my super majestic tinsel villa is a house of '*white collar dirts*', who are appearing so clean to the world; but are actually corroding and making the country hollow like a hidden parasite."

Seeing the rage in my words and on my face all went quiet, but piercing that silence my mom slapped me hard, but in all these hot talks we forgot that my sweet granny was seeing all these, and so on hearing and knowing it all, that only true soul in that fake house fainted, seeing her serious all discussions were dissolved and she was admitted in the hospital.

To see my lifeline in the crisis of her own life struggling with those oxygen chamber, I was feeling like nothing real was left with me, so in my acute pain I thought of my love Vicky. The only real thing in my life.

But his number was busy when I was feeling dead without granny and my love, but thank God suddenly nurse came with a small relief that granny was out of danger. I thanked to god and was able to sleep.

Then in the next good thing that happened was, it was a call from Vicky and his voice was as if he was boozing or was very much tired.

And he told me that he needs me, and with a smile I replied that I was always there for him, and I said that even I wanted to talk to him about something very serious so was trying his number but it was busy.

He said it was his brother's call and I sai Okay.

Then he further told me that he wasn't well so would hear me out later. At his sad state I didn't want to give stress to him burdening him with my problems and thought when granny would be fine, I'd meet him and would ask him to marry me soon, so that I couldn't fall prey to the plan of trapping Siddharth .

So to calm him with all my love I said him bye and to take care... and that I loved him a lot"

And after this, I left for the church because I was missing granny that time the most and in the church today I was alone without granny but was still feeling some relief of satisfaction before god and sensing the light smell of fresh and my favourite lilies outside the church, this was the only pure thing I had grown up feeling with my granny.

So to pray for her I went in that big and silent church where I was going since my childhood with her, and there I was felt like mother Maryam is saying to me in the voice of granny and even the sentences were same which my granny always used to preach me during my childhood.

May be it were my granny's words or her preaching in me so this fake world was still unable to murder my soul for its fake glitters.

I closed my eyes and in a series I was remembering my childhood and was hearing those words of granny, which I was feeling like mother Maryam was saying to me.

"*Whenever & where ever life goes, the only thing that lasts till the end is values, and those values only bring the real satisfaction of happiness*".

Realizing those words to be true I felt, now mother Maryam was quiet in my imagination and that small Ishika was left alone in her big world and granny was no where with that small kid, that little Ishika was crying yet granny wasn't coming to her.

I was scared and opened my eyes and that moment grand paa called me to say granny that is no more with us, hearing him from church to hospital I ran like a mad.

But to capture that painful moment and to question me, it was still important for media I don't know how they could have traced me that evening there in that abandoned area?

There I saw granny was lying down in relief, as if she was happy to be away from this false world, as if she was in relief away from all her pains. I wasn't even able to cry but I went closer to her and when I touched her she was all cold.

I couldn't bear it and was broken hard with tears, I was least interested to look at the world around, when the ground of my world wasn't there with me anymore; to support me when everything was false and this way my lovely granny took her exit from the stage of life and this way Eliza Singh was buried deep inside.

Without her, I felt lost. After a day, we had some religious ceremony at our tinsel ville so that people can come and pray, so that God blesses her soul to rest in peace.

For my tinsel villa relation with mighty media was very old and I don't know all those peoples who came to pray for my granny were actually praying for her or were showing themselves to media?

But all were sharing all good memories related to her with media, even my mom too was doing the same. But I think my mom was always so busy that she was never able to look up on granny well under the smudges of her eye makeup.

Even today too she had selected a light coloured suit and a light makeup for this day and to bring tears in her eyes even more than me wasn't a big deal for that great actress.

But according to me that ceremony was a waste because for a lady like my granny heaven is for sure because all her real and sweet memories she carved and left behind were like those of an angel.

Now a week had passed. All were back to their work, dadu was practicing those powerful speeches which were prepared by the beaurocrats of our country and he was learning it well, so that no mistake happens.

As it happened once, that our hardly literate rulers before whom we bow , didn't noticed and while in his speech in the vote of appeal he started reading those of budgets.

And on the other side my mom was practicing dialogue and was busy with her schedule, dad was mostly out and nanoo was holding all his meetings. So this way all were back to their normal & busy life.

But for me to get back to practice for my passion was still tough, and then one night after dinner for the first time my mom came to my room, I was happy to see her she again kissed me loudly to show her love; but I was never able to feel that real love of warmth in her big kiss which I used to felt with small affection of my granny.

Then she spoke to me about now I should come out of my sorrows, granny had a wonderful life and now must be in peace in heaven. So now I should focus on my life, I found logic in her practical words.

Then she asked me to practice well for my show next day, I was quiet for that, then she reminded that tomorrow I would have to meet Siddharth, hearing this tears filled my eyes and I held hands of my mom and said her "but I love Vicky"!

"And it's nothing childish. He also loves me too"

But my mom was silent, then I told her that I couldn't think of any other man because our relationship has gone beyond, and we had moment of intimacy, at this my mom said so calmly like all time.

That in young age sometime somewhere the moments are such that a guy and girl can't resist and share intimate moments but it doesn't mean they have to be together forever.

Then my mom said that the best thing about Vicky and my intimacy was that, the media was still unaware and I was able to made it safely and I am not pregnant else the visit to the gynecologist could have been a risk and would have been problematic.

Hearing her, I was broken and said, "Sorry mom, I am not so practical like you that even after seeing dad loving some other girl you are okay! And not even like dad, who doesn't ever care to know where you had been last night".

At this my mom was silent and in anger she left my room. I expected that she will slap me for this again, but this time too she again managed to be cool somehow and I never know how.

That moment I realized my mom had never been to her daughter as a mom, rather she was always as a practical Ratika Gaur Singh with some most logical ideas.

After all this I thought that now I should must ask Vicky to marry me before that master plan again comes to their mind, which they had temporarily left because granny was inactive permanently.

So I called Vicky and he said he was sorry to hear about my granny but in my tough time he was trying to make me strong to deal it on my own, so he said that "he planned this treatment modality and didn't call me or supported me, because he wanted that I should come out from the memories of granny myself without him".

Without thinking much I told him that I wanted him to marry me, at this he said "What? Now?" My granny just left and then my shows was at its peak, marriage would destroy my popularity.

So I told him that I would meet him and would explain him and after knowing all the traps and plans, he would also marry me no matter if the time isn't right, because love knows no time or anything.

Inspite of my unhealed and for ever green wound after the death of granny, I was able to feel some drops of happiness and it was only because of my love Vicky. So today I was prepared well with all required documents for a court marriage , thus early morning in a somewhat a better dresse I left for Vicky.

On the way I was thinking that unlikely to the master plan of my super power family, I will be Mrs. Vicky in front of the world today before the evening show, so to save our fake majesty titanic I wouldn't have to sell out myself in the hand of any Siddharth.

With this I reached his home, his guard was surprised to see me early, he knew who I was, so he did not stop or questioned me.

But I felt awkward that why he wasn't trying to stop me. Without thinking much, with a smile I entered his house, I knew It was early so I was sure Vicky must be sleeping.

So I stepped straight to his bed room to surprise him, but I wasn't knowing that in a chunk of second I would be getting the biggest surprise of my life ever.

With a smile I opened the door because I knew

the code already 777 and opened my mouth so say Vicky, but was only able to say Vi...

In the hazy dim lights of night bulb I was able to recognize him, but the pillow snuggled tightly by him; had a golden skin and soon I moved towards the bed, but my feet got tangled on some cloth on floor; I bend to picked it up and found it to be the garments of a girl.

Seeing that, the whole picture was clear to me in that hazy light, each corner of the room from the door to the covered curtain of windows; were telling the story of the night.

The small amount of left over wine in the glass, those folds on bed sheet and the warm sounds of two breathes resonating as one because they were close together and it all made me to imagine how they made love last night.

I was thinking the passion meant for my love and was for some other slim fair and straight hair creature last night, with all these in that silent room ; my conscious were hijacked and I never noticed that when the tears in my painful sigh went audible to separate and woke up those two bare bodies.

The rays of sun that time didn't just had lighten up the room, but it had removed the mask of Vicky and had let me to see the real picture of that man; the one whom I loved. Above all, cared more than all and had trusted the most unfortunately.

But today he sold it all on bed with someone, seeing me that girl covered herself with the bed sheet and took an exit, and Vicky was speechless. My silent eyes were asking him why? And in anger I exploded on him and said.

"So it was this important work, so this man

was trying to pretend so great, to avoid me because he wanted to help me to come out of the pain of my granny's death.

And that's why he was refusing marriage and was scared like a teared up man to hold my man before this world".

To hear all these he was silent and then started laughing and said to me,

"You too have learned to act like your mom, to give a speech like your grand paa and to play on bed like your father, but from them why you couldn't learn to be practical"?

Saying this he quoted example of my mom and asked me to learn to be practical like her , who didn't care to see the video of her hubby loving some other girl, similarly I too shouldn't try to act so traditional, to see me sleeping bare with some other girl.

At this I slapped him and said "I loved you damn it! Unfortunately! So I didn't know what being practical meant?" At this he laughed again and said ,

"But I never said I love you too, may be sometime while loving you, I would have said 'love you baby' but that doesn't meant love. Because Vicky don't believe in love".

And with a smile he said that whenever i came to him he kissed me and loved me and i never even stopped him, because i too was liking it all, similarly last night that girl came to his room with drink, and by herself she offered him and he couldn't stopped him self."

His words shattered me into pieces, and more than him, I hated myself. Why I trusted him so much? Why I loved him so much? Actually I was just a body for him and love means just to fuck for him.

He was still bare on bed under the bed sheet. But I didn't feel like looking at him again. May be my broken heart still had some love for him, because he was my first and true love and with tears in my eyes and pains in my heart, I left his home and drove my car and went to some bar.

There, it was a dirty crowd, smokes and were men turned into wolves over the song, that was being played inside was of my mom's item song and the semi naked girls were moving there body on its note.

May be in that darkness no one could noticed me. Or may be they all were lost in some other world. I too was in the worst of my pain and so I thought with these alcohols, I would be able to get over it.

If the wounds of missing my granny was green, then the pain of my broken heart had made me lifeless in few minutes, and so I took pegs on peg endlessly beyond count.

That time lost in my pains and sedation, I didn't noticed that when the crowd of people and camera surrounded me, the star by birth Miss Ishika Gaur Sing, and I don't remember exactly but I could notice that crowd was asking how me Ishika is there? And my painful eyes was just able to give them a plain look.

Today I had no guard and none to take me away from them, because with a plan of marriage I left home alone. And alas! Now I was left with nothing.

Suddenly I noticed a hand with big nails coated in red nail paints and bangles in them, dragged me away from that crowd, I was lost and wasn't knowing what was happening? My sense were fainted and that young lady said seeing me, "I must have fallen prey to loving the wrong one" to this I smiled at her. Then she said the love of a wrong man ends a woman so wrongly, and so she doesn't love a man and rather loves a women"

Saying this when she hugged me tight before I knew, and started kissing me.

Soon I felt that something behind me was vibrating, so I removed her hands from my back, took out my cell phone from my back pocket and I smiled to see that for the first time my mom was worried that were I am? since a long on the day of my show when I had to met someone.

But actually that call wasn't for my care, but it was because she was feeling humiliated to see me boozing in a cheap club and she was shouting at me that what the hell I was doing?

At that moment when I was getting destroyed in all possible ways. The world was able to see it live, and again it was that same media who had followed me before my birth; was following me again but this time to abuse me.

That moment on all channels I was cursed. Hearing all these from my mom, I put on my jacket back taken out by that lady, and parting those crowd I left that place.

But had not been to my home; rather had been to the stage of my dream grand show where today I had to perform for my passion video.

Vicky was there with his band, but today my actual passion to stretch me there on stage wasn't music nor even my love, rather it was just the passion of my insanity.

Seeing me, the majestic and powerful Ishika Gaur Singh in her worst already destroyed state the whole crowd turned towards me ignoring that tempting note of Vicky.

But without caring about anything, I went to the stage directly and took the mic and all music was muted itself, and for the first time in the worst of my worst tangled hairs, torn dress, swollen face, red eyes having black tears because of spoiled eye makeups and spread lipstick, the audience was in a great shock of silence.

I opened my lips but not to sing rather to say and I speak to the mass, "Thanks everyone for coming, inspite of knowing that the born super star the power girl in herself, the young sensation of music Ishika Gaur Singh! The fusion of all powers of nation. Was boozing and then doing wild fantasies with someone in a bar. Yet you all took the pain to come here to make me feel like I am still the star, and then after seeing me here you all ignored the wonderful music of Mr. Hot Dude Vicky and went silent to greet me. To prove that before Ishika Gaur Singh who is now destroyed, is yet more than any Vicky Mickey or whatever....

Yes, what you all saw live was true, but you all just saw just a part of it. I was taking pegs on pegs there and then I was in a prison of kisses of a girl. Yes, she was a girl so don't confuse saying the person with long hair and who was that girl and why she did that I don't know that.

One thing that I just know is that her kisses wasn't as passionate as Vicky's.

Yes. Vicky, this same guy playing music here, is really a hot dude whom I started loving truly with my heart.

And so a few times had surrendered myself to him, thinking he too loved me and so I made love, thinking real love didn't need any commitment papers to be signed and forgot that's a sin actually.

But for this hot guy, having bully beards and piercings have no difference between love and time pass, heart and body. Yes! and this hot dude says it all to be a practical rather than emotional.

But I never knew what being practical is? I just know this morning I left my house without the blessing of my late granny; following my heart to marry this hot dude, because I was left with no option .

Otherwise I was asked to sell myself to a rich investor present here. Some Mr. Siddharth to save the pillars of my majestic tinsel villa. A fusion of business, politics, Bollywood and cricket that is supporting the royal roof of my tinsel villa.

But ... alas! What I saw today had shattered me, this hot Vicky dude was bare and bold on bed the same way with some slim, short and golden skin girl. And so I too, the born star, no in fact the only super star of the nation, Ishika Gaur Singh decided to be practical without caring about the media and crowd.

So I too followed my heart for the first time to booze and then again followed my heart to speak out something that is embedded pained unbearably.

This morning I thought from this stage, I'll sing being Mrs. Vicky as I planned, but today here I am giving an unprepared speech being a destroyed star. "

The crowd was listening to me with more silence today. It wasn't shouting in my support as it had always cheered and shouted in my shows.

And this way I was again in topics and debates and had some group in my support, some were anti and some were neutral.

My huge family told the media that the doctors said, "I had a serious depression after my granny left and so had nervous break down".

After that I don't know either media was supporting me or cursing me, because I didn't have the courage to see any news channels or read the news paper; as I planned to check them out after the success of my show.

I didn't know about the world but in my own home I was alone. Mom was saying how I could be so careless, dad as usual wasn't at home like my past 18 years & I wasn't knowing where he was.

Grand paa was tensed that such an episode by me during the election would ruin his image and nanoo was depressed that now Siddharth wouldn't help him and his money will not turn into white money to attract shares.

So my dad on phone might had suggested all to send me abroad until it all settles, and so today that same Ishika Gaur Singh whose each move used to be in lime light and caught attention, was hidden inside her own home and was planned to be sent abroad secretly.

Really! This time the plan of my destiny showed me that, some time life doesn't go according to our plan, and my life who had always shown me its kindest face today had shown its most cruel face.

I didn't know what was in the folds of my destiny? Was that an end of a chapter or the starting of a new? I was totally unaware of it. I was just going with the flow, I just knew that next day early morning I would be leaving for some place in Europe.

But I was just praying there that I shouldn't be identified and wont be in spotlights again.

This way the super girl, the sensational born star had totally submitted herself to the hands of her destiny, I was broken deep inside and was destroyed in all ways.

I was missing granny, so that in her lap I could have cried and could have released my pains, but now she was also far away from me. And those who were around in that big and majestic tinsel villa were dipped in their own life.

I didn't know where my parents were? Who had already paid a lot of the money for their daughter so far, yet they where out of the scene. Even my mom knew that tomorrow I would be gone but she wasn't with me at that time too, even my dad wasn't caring where I would go.

I know grand paa and nanoo all were angry with me, so they were sending me away so far. I was scared deep inside but more than all this I was sad that why didn't any of them, those who were my own, come to ask me that why I did so ? what I did and why I took such extreme steps? . Because I had never taken such an extreme step ever before.

But inspite of consoling me, may be it was more important for them to console the mass and media, to curb those gossip about me and my power title of Gaur Sing. It was hard for me to check out media that was continuously showing my story since my lavish birth to the insane destruction.

And today I was compared to many such destroyed stars. It was hard for me to see and believe, that it was all the same channels who used to interview me, used to hype me for each of my moves, was today cursing me so badly as if I had broken all the rules and l have destroyed the whole world.

The mass that used to say the best about me and used to follow me, was today burning my pictures and were spitting on me as if I was the only slut on the fair name of this Indian society.

Seeing this I switched of the television. It was like so difficult for me even to breathe; I was knowing that I am finished and so all this happening to me. I realized that how true it is, that this world never supports the waste and craps and so nothing was there to support me too.

In the blessing of this power title Gaur Singh, Ishika was vanished in the dark crisis, today this boon has become the doom for me, and in this time I had no friend, no love & no family to support me, I was felt like changing my identity before this world forever.

Chapter 5 - The transformation....

Few minutes were left for me to leave and few hours were still there for the dawn to completely brighten up the sky. I was packed with a little because I already had loads of memories with me.

There I wasn't going to be in the limelight so repeating dresses wasn't a big thing for me. Though I was going there for treatment but don't know why I was feeling like that I was leaving everything of my world behind forever.

Cars were honking and I had to leave. As I turned to leave, I felt happiness to see my parents at my door. I moved towards them to hug them tight; but before I could do so, my dad said, "I should avoid media in every possible ways, and my mom asked me to check for my ATM card and tickets ".

And so without hugging them I just managed to smile and said thanks. It was all well arranged as ever, but I was unlucky enough to get a smile back from them, may be they were still so angry with me.

While going out I saw grand paa on the gate he looked at me and waved bye, I just touched his feet to earn his blessing but he was silent unlike ever before. Since a long I was waiting to turn 18 to vote for his party, but when I was 18 now, I was going with so much pain.

Tears were in my eyes, but may be it were invisible to all, grand paa told me that all is arranged and this time I had to be careful.

What was going in my destroyed mind, broken heart and teary eyes it was all invisible to the world that time; and this way I took the private flight and so this way unseen from this world I left my old world of glamour where I was born and welcomed.

From there I arrived to a far off world which wasn't of my own and with no hope, no desire and no dream, a lifeless body was just moving on the flow of life .

I was brought to some place in interior of Europe near Austria. The moment I stepped out into the town for the first time, I felt the freedom, no crowd was following me and no media was there.

In the beauty of that small place with flowers and clouds I was like a free bird, and according to the address I reached the rehabilitation center for my treatment.

There I was questioned for around an hour with the experienced and most renowned doctors, who used to bring the broken and destroyed people like me back to life.

But they found me fine and said I was an easy case to treat, for them I was just a case, a case of depression and nervous breakdown. They were sure they would treat me back to life easily, but they did not know that my life itself was my disease so how would they treat me?

In my views in order to treat me, they needed to kill me and then to make to born again. In that center I was following the routine of sleeping, waking up & eating etc. right from my morning walk to my medicine dose at bed all were planned there.

And this way almost a month passed, they used to take me to all the beautiful places so that I could restart loving my life again. Those places were like the ones where my mom had been for her shooting.

With this they said I was well now, and could go back, I didn't know I was well or not. But yes, far from my world here in the peace; where I was a common girl of the crowd unidentified and so I was in little peace.

So from that center after my so called treatment, I went to a small hotel; because in big hotel I didn't want any link of my old world. As in bigger hotels, the risk of getting identified were high.

The money in my ATM was ample for me to live my life well, in that hotel apart from eating, sleeping, watching television and net surfing I had nothing more to do in Europe. Internet was newly introduced that time.

After a month, I saw news of my country. In Indian news my family still covered the headlines. But now they were discussing where was Ishika Gaur Singh on her 18th birthday? And my family had sealed their lips over it.

So media and mass were making their own conclusion and were giving judgments like, "Ishika is doing remorse of her sins, some were saying she is punished for other sins too."

Like this there many expert comments from numerous expert's mouths, and with all this, the majestic tinsel villa was sinking further.

Now my dad wasn't the captain of the Indian cricket team, nor my mom was the lead role actress of any block buster, nor my grand paa was having majority in his party, nor the notes of nanoo were able to become white.

And the only thing that I knew, that still in the bad times too my parents were just a social husband & wife like the past 19 years.

I don't know how without love they were together since a long without any argument, anger and fight like a couple? Or may be there was no love and it was all planned and practical for the lavishness: so they were together so well as a perfect couple for the society.

Seeing this all in news and thinking all these, I understood that the way luck attracts luck and fortune attracts fortune. Similarly problems attract problems. And a single wrong move, sometime blow out the long span of labour.

Now I was scared to return back to that world where all knew me and unluckily this time with a bad name. I did not also have the option to stay there in Europe any more longer, I was helpless; as if in the middle of an ocean and didn't know how to swim.

I was feeling like to die, but I thought sooner or later my death again will be in the news and the gossips and comments about my death without knowing the reality will not let me to rest in peace even after my death.

I was feeling like changing my identity. With this I started searching on net how to change identity? And I found many people some changing their name, some were migrating, some were changing their face, some were even changing their sex, and few were changing their name and religion .

It all made me imbalanced, I was thinking that world calls these people mad; but in my views they were strong actually.

At least with the change of their identity they were able to get the second option, apart from suicide to restart their life on their own way with peace. Sometime back I was feeling like to end up my life but now I too had an option.

It was a big decision for me to change my identity and to cut off myself from my actual world , but it was the only way for me left .

So I thought better than dying in suffocation, I should die as Ishika Gaur Singh and reborn as a new common girl because the real Ishika had died long back under the suffocation of her super power title Gaur Singh.

It wasn't so easy for me, to bury myself with our own hand and yet be alive. So in pain, tears were again in my eyes. I was looking up at myself perhaps for the last time in the mirror with the face I was born with had grown up and was known with it.

I loved face of Ishika and the world too had loved this face a lot, and some time excess of love, even turns to be toxic and so this time because of this world I had to change my face.

So I planned some thing, I kept all my important documents in a bag and went out taking a car in the country side. I already had paid enough to the concerned person so he let me do what I wanted without any single word.

Intentionally I made a small accident and got bruised on face my self and put fire in car, so that my bag having documents gets burned.

Then from there I called doctors, whom I have already met and set for the plastic surgery of my face, and so I had been straight to them.

A team of expert plastic surgeons took my images and other medical reports in a series, and interrogated me that my face is good and pleasing only has few bruises of accident, so why I want to change?

For this I was able to reply only a sentence "I want to reborn in all possible ways", may be this sentence was enough to tell them that its my physiological need, and so they took me to the big and sterilized surgery room, for the last time I saw my fair, round dimpled face with small nose, lips and grey eyes.

Neither did they asked me like whom I want to look like, nor did I tell, may be they got it from my expressions, that I don't had any more desire with my life.

I remember the things in that room till I was anaesthetized, after that I was floating in some other world and I don't remember for how long that surgery went on.

After many hours I opened my eyes, I was feeling some pain, I felt like I was waking up after a long time. I saw a sweet nurse sitting beside me. She smiled looking at me, and told me "for some days it will pain, soon the marks from my face and pain will go on its own but till then I have to be very regular with the dosages of medicines".

I was quietly listening her, my old cute face was still in my mind; but still I wanted to see my new one and may be that nurse noticed my expression, and so she handed me a mirror.

My face was in my mind, but still my eyes were seeing a new face of mine, after eighteen years for the first time I was seeing a new me.

Now it was oval slim face,it wasn't having that

baby cheeks of sweet Ishika, now my eyes were big and golden , I was fairer, my lips were bigger and nose was more chiseled and narrow.

May be I was more beautiful now or lesser prettier I don't know. But that moment I felt doctors are like second god; who had really made me reborn somehow with the best of their work.

With tears in my eyes and smile on my face I thanked them, tears were because in a few hours I was having a new face and my old face was erased, and I was able to smile because I thought atleast like this I was saved, from the thoughts of suicide. Because to kill yourself with your own hand was more tough according to me it required more courage.

In around a week those marks and pains were reduced notably and I was discharged from there and thank God I had enough money to make the doctors stay lip sealed about my face change surgery; really! Some time money can buy anything.

In these days nor anyone from tinsel villa contacted me, nor I contacted them, but I was worried that how with the burnt documents of Ishika Gaur Singh I will go back? Because the visa period of Europe was about to end.

So just made a complaint in police that in an accident I lost all my documents and had my face destroyed. So had these surgeries done and doctors too had spoken in my support; as they were already set.

Thank god sometime money proves to be the mightiest of all, and this way with power of currency, somehow I managed a new documents with a new name.

I just replaced one letter of I with A and from

Ishika I renamed me as Ashika, and was able to come back to my country, with a new face and a new identity. Where no one knew this transformation from Ishika to Ashika....

Chapter 6 - Life after my rebirth....

After around a couple of months I was back to my country, this re entry was after a rebirth wasn't a simple journey to me, in these two months Ashika had buried Ishika, some where deep where no power world, no camera, no media could have reached.

Because after the death of that born sensational star, a simple girl was reborn. These two months not just had made me more fair, slim and more beautiful but my mind was more matured, but my heart was now just an organ, there were no dreams in those pretty eyes & all hopes and desires were also buried.

I had transformed myself to new simple girl with the same mind, the same heart used to miss sometime that prettiest and cutest Ishika, who never stopped speaking and dreaming. Who was innocent yet full of glamour.

I was still missing myself and it was tough for me to accept myself as Ashika, because Ashika was yet new to me in her looks in her ways, though Ashika was re created by this destiny only , but the situations made Ashika so silent and matured like this.

Yet Ashika was selected by me for myself, so didn't have any complain. But now the broken me had no words to speak, no aim to hope & no dream to work for all times, all were lost in suffocation of pain and silence. I was living because I just had to be alive, and now even after trying a million times I couldn't be the same, because once you are broken deeply you are changed forever.

Now I was back to my country where I was born with a grand welcome, but now with my changed face I was among the common mass. My new name and new thoughts had already burnt all my old identity and after coming back I destroyed my ATM card too because I never wanted to be traced and go back to that world which I had left a far behind.

I used to think about my family, but then I thought they haven't spoken to me since many weeks, and yet they are inactive means for the sake of their image; they haven't made any complaint in police about my whereabouts. Also, elections were at its peak and hence no one wanted their reputation to be at stake.

In my mother land, I chose Benaras to live, because it was a small town, where peoples were coming more for the pious job of worshiping and not for movies shots and parties.

But being out for the first time on my own, without a single penny, straight from the life of lavishness to the world of simplicity and struggling life; I realized how tough it is.

Now I was in the need of that first and foremost thing that we need to pass our life, is shelter and meal. For that we need money and the quality of that shelter and meal is determined by penny in our pocket.

Money its importance and the sacrifices we go through to earn it, who could have witnessed it better than me?

I was so lonely in this new place without any money to be able to spend. First night was spent with the ladies worshiping and sleeping on the floor of the temple.

For the first time I was trying to sleep at the crowded public place alone. The place wasn't even cleaned and it had a foul smell, yet I had no place better than a crowded temple. Next day I freshened up myself with the water of the holy Ganges, and was feeling so hungry but soon I was proven to be lucky to see some rich people, who were doing charity of providing food to the people in the temple.

From them I was able to get two samosas and jalebi, after taking the food of charity I was recalling my breakfast till two months ago; that was perhaps the most royal breakfast of the country. Now this breakfast of charity by people who were either trying to lessen their sins or were trying to increase their good deeds by feeding me and people like me there.

But one thing I liked about this charity that it was done in a concealed manner, not like what my mother was doing with cameras and media, not actually to please God but to charm the mass for the sake of her publicity.

After sleeping and getting fresh with splash from the water of holy ganges and a breakfast of charity, I regained some energy and thought that it would be better to look up for some work to get a shelter and to arrange for meal.

But I didn't know where to start. And how to start. But sometimes God helps us so fast during our worst or may be in that city of temples at Benaras, God hears and respond faster.

So a lady beside me woke up who was sleeping on the news paper on the floors of temple, and on the right time my eyes struck at the place where it was written, "REQUIRED" in capital letter, I read that paragraph and found that in some school a teacher cum hostel warden was needed for a girls hostel.

I checked it and found that the news paper was of Sunday, and today it was Monday morning 7am and interview was at 9am, so seeing the address I managed rushed to that place, and entered for the interview.

It was a small government girls school, where the other candidates were also there in the que like me for that job.

But they all had big files in their hand, unlike me and that was the file of their degrees, it made me worried; yet I prayed and after two girls, it came my turn to enter for the interview.

I gave a well introduction of mine, "I am Ashika. I lost my family and my degrees and everything in an accident in Europe" , and showed them the copy of complaint paper which I had made there and all the medical reports, may be my introduction had impressed them. That time the costly education of my elite schooling was proven to be effective. Or may be they pitied me. And asked me what I could do for the school and the girls at hostel?

At this I replied in the same impressive way, and It all wasn't made up answer, rather it was the real me coming out, because after so many days I was talking to someone.

I said, "I have lost everything in the accident, so if I will get this job, I will live here as my home, I will love the girls as my sisters, at school I will teach them literature; but at hostel I will play, will teach them singing, dancing painting etc. With them I will share their problems and will guide them to shape them to a nice person as their elder sister. If needed I will clean up this place as we clean our home because now i have no home and family"

With this they said I could join from tomorrow. On hearing this I was so happy that my throat was heavy and eyes were wet and with a heavy voice I asked them that, if I could join from today? "Because if you will let me to join from today , then I will be saved off from sleeping on the floors of temple again this night", hearing me they smiled and said "sure why not". I was so happy to hear this, because for the first time in my life, on my own I was able to arrange food and shelter for myself.

With my small bag I entered the hostel, from inside the campus of school was so big, it was an old building, was appearing like it was made during the time of British.

The attendant took me to the girls hostel that was behind the school, my room was first in the rows of rooms. In total there were 20 rooms in which around 40 girls were there in the hostel.

The old and simple attendant on the way explained me the things about the place and the room in which the hostel warden had to live.

It was a medium sized room, with plenty of air and sunshine, but it was appearing that the abandoned room, wasn't cleaned up since long.

On its wooden table and shelf there was lot of dust, spider webs, the narrow bed had a thin mattress covered with dust; on which there were cockroaches.

On the ground there were rats and it was all smelling foul, and there was a small ceiling fan tangled with webs of spiders. I switched on the fan but found at its full speed it was moving so slowly that I was able to count its blade.

In my life I have never seen a room like that. Its appearance made my appearance grief. At this that attendant said me to not worry. He would clean up the things . At this I thanked him..

In that month of June I was soaked with sweat for the first time in my life. I asked the attendant to clean it all; till then I went and freshened up.

Then the room was in its cleanup process and I was in the interaction process with the girls. It was the primary school so all the girls were up to the age of 14 at the max.

They all were simple girls of middle class families, all were looking different than the girls of my school. They all had oil in their hair and some had pierced nose. But the best thing was that in a few minutes they all were friendly to me.

I kept my small bag in the room of the girl who was the head girl of the hostel; may be because she was the most senior and sincere among all.

She offered me a glass of water and I had cold water to drink in her room taken out from the earthen pot drinking in a steel glass, that too after such a long in that heat. So I felt some relief.

From there I went for a bath, and for the first time in my life I was using a common bathroom allotted for 10 girls, it wasn't dirty but wasn't even a single percent of the bathrooms which I had used so far.

Water was hot in the tap because summer were

scorching. For the first time I washed my dress with detergents that's why my hands were may be itching, Because I had a habit of using the mildest and the best hand washes ever.

For a long time I was thinking about my past life till two months back. I was wondering if I had taken an immature and fool step? The worst decision of my life? Would I be able to survive with these struggles? Should I go back?

These all were in my mind, suddenly I closed my eyes to imagine what my life would be if I went back. What I saw was a lot of media asking me why and how, why I changed my self? Where I was? How I did this all? What made me to do all these? And for all the why, who, what when etc. I would have to be speechless, and then in that big house among my own people I would be lonely in that show world of glamour. My career will be nothing nor I will be able to do any thing of my own.

With all these thoughts, I opened my eyes and realized; that the world where I have seen the best and the most cherished moments of my life, returning there back meant to face the worse of the worst.

At least whatever I am doing now was much better, because I didn't have to answer to any one, no media was there to trace my life, I could do something of my own, and most importantly here I didn't have to feel lonely among my own people; because I knew here none is in any relation with me, so here I am not alone in the crowd of my own the way I had been after my granny.

With all these thoughts I was out from the bathroom after a long and went to my room which was now cleaned and was absolutely dust free, no spider webs, rather it had having a fresh bed sheet, pillow and curtain.

Few girls helped me to unpack and arrange my small bag having some dresses, foot wears and other things of necessity. The room was now in some what living condition and I thanked God that he helped me to find a safe roof in this new town. Otherwise last night was pathetic and so unsafe for a young and lonely girl to sleep alone. Then I had lunch, I was so hungry that I ate simple daal chawal with curd, salads, vegetable and papad and after that I slept for a long. In the eve I was woken up for tea by a lady. She was dark and short. A simple lady, who had cleaned my room. She was the cleaner of the hostel.

Silently and lost in nothing when I was taking hot sips of tea, a sweet young girl appearing of around 7 to 8 years came to me.

She was looking so pretty, her face had made her to look different from all the other girls, and she sat with me and said I am so beautiful and I look like her mom.

I thanked her and said you are also very pretty your mom must be proud of you. At this she said; "Yes! She is very proud on me".

Then she asked me where my home was? I was quiet at this, and instead of answering that innocent, I asked her where her home was and that her mom must be missing her there.

Then with such simplicity in her words she said, "My mom doesn't miss me that's why, many years back she went to the house of God to bring my dad back from there, my dad went their after being injured at a border fight as a brave army man of the nation, but after going there they both have forgotten me, and have't come back".

Her innocent words made my eyes wet, I was left with no words and hugged her, and then she again said that soon she will also go to the house of God to meet her parents, I had nothing to reply her, so I offered her some biscuits, and asked her name, and that pretty girl said her name was Guria, and I smiled hearing her name because she was prettier than any doll to deserve the name Guria. And that moment I felt I am not just the one with problems in my life.

She too smiled and talked to me for a long, and in that small girl soon I found a simple and an innocent friend, which I could never have in my life.

Next day I went to the school and I was the class teacher of standard 3rd. I began with the attendance, introduction of all students and my introduction to them, and then taught all the subjects. During lunch time I had lunch at the school canteen.

For the first day it was a bit tough for me to control the class and to interact with other teachers, but with time it all became a habit and then like this a month passed and I got my first salary of eight thousand rupees.

In that hostel I got food shelter and some work to do, so that amount was of no use for me, so with my new family of the young girls of hostel, I went out and took some dress for me, some gifts for all the girls and packed some tasty plates of vegetarian and non vegetarian food for all of us .

In the evening with all the girls, we had good food after a long time, like this I was adjusting there slowly.

One day Guria fell ill. The doctor examined her and said she is having some breathing problem, so everyday she should be taken for walks in early morning in fresh air.

In these few months I had developed a deep connection with Guria, so from that day I started taking her for the walks in the field behind the school soon after the sunrise.

She used to walk everyday morning and I used to see the young and old couples walking together and parents playing with their children.

Seeing all these I used to think simple people have simple life meant for their family which is pretty sweet and big peoples have complicated life; which is meant for every thing except their own people. And I realized that truth and simplicity were the things that I was lacking in my life.

I had everything in that life except love of my own people. But among these strangers, I got the feeling of love, care and a true relation.

When I was thinking and comparing all these, I saw a middle aged lady with a white puppy on her lap was sitting beside me and after her walk she was taking juice and was feeding dry fruits to her puppy too. That rich dog was lucky to have a gold chain in his neck.

Soon a small boy came to that lady begging for food, but she neglected him and the dog too started barking at him, as if dog was telling him to get lost! How dare he!

Maybe the hunger of that small boy made him go a bit crazy, so he snatched the juice and dry fruits from the hands of that lady and ran. The lady left her dog behind him to teach him a lesson. That hungry, weak and poor boy fell after running fast and was crying and shouting save me! Please some one save me, help.

Soon I saw a young tall and fair guy, came running

breaching the crowd like an angel and stood in front of the dog as a protective sheath for that small boy, his rage and toughness was enough to make the barking dog go silent. He helped him stand back and rest of guys in the crowd were watching the scene and he saved that scared small boy.

Then the lady came back and the man who saved the boy told her to take her juice and peanuts back. She could feed her dog and can make him to wear a gold chain but couldn't give some penny to this poor boy.

At this that lady was quiet, then I saw my small Guria go to that small boy who was begging and gave him her apples to eat, at this the scared boy hesitated to take it but when that man insisted him, he took it from her, then that tall man thanked Guria with a smile.

Like this with school, hostel and morning walks, months passed and summers turned to winters and in these months, all that was common and stable with my life was school, hostel, girls and that tall guy at the ground whom I was seeing everyday but we never had interacted. May be after Vicky I was scared of boys.

After this whatever time I used to get I used to write inspiring thoughts that I had collected from my life in my diary. Everyday in school I used to see how with love fathers used to bring their kids to school and mothers used to come to take them back. In parents teacher meet both parents would be together asking the teachers about their kids and during annual days those parents would take pride on the performance of their kid.

Seeing these I felt how my childhood missed these small and precious moments. Today it was 28th of October. Seeing this date my eyes were fixed on the calendar with pains at the midnight. It was birthday of Ishika Gaur Singh, meaning it was my birthday. The most awaited day of my life, When I was like a princess in demand and whole nation was watching and blessing me.

Remembering my birthday, the only person I was really missing was my granny. And dipped in my pain, I was sitting on the chair of my room as still, hostel was also empty because of deepawali vacations.

With all these thoughts I do not remember when I slept. And at 1am, I woke up again with a bad dream of my past life, so for some change I went to the TV room of the hostel and opened news channel to know what media was showing for on the birthday of Ishika Gaur Singh. What people of tinsel villa were saying? And today what the mass was discussing.

My guess was right. On all news channels it was again Ishika after a long interval of 7months, and I was shocked to see that for this world, I was declared dead. In media, a young and smart journalist was expressing grief over my death, as if he was such a well wisher of mine.

Headlines said that Ishika couldn't see her 19th birthday. There were questions asking what made her to leave this world secretly? How and when she left this world etc. It was that same media, who was cursing me few months back when I was broken and had expressed my pain before the world, when I was the worst prey of my golden destiny.

Today in the same media was shocked to see, that my nanoo who just had contributed for charity actually to made his notes white but he was showing he did it to provide peace to my soul over my fake death.

Now he was successful to make his tie with Siddharth and they were opening a charitable school for poor on my name and on the day of my birthday. My grandpa was going to inaugurate it may be to glorify his party, and like every time my mom was in the gurudwara with media to donate and to pray that may God give peace to my soul, and like every time my dad was absent from this scene too like he was absent from my life always.

Seeing the news of my death, being alive and the politics over it for self gains shook the ground of my existence and I felt my powerful family of Gaur Singh was yet so influential that if it would have really tried, they could have traced me, but may be they didn't try and that's why so easily they accepted that I was dead.

The day when Ishika was turning 19, world was mourning over her death and then Ashika was just 7months old at the age of nineteen. I always used to imagine and had hope against the hopes; in these months that some day my family will miss me, will be able to find me, and will come and hug me and will ask me to come back with love.

Though I had left my world myself, it was true that the bond of blood relations sometimes made me day dream, may be some time even the loveliest dreams do come true, but my family will come and hug me was more than any dream! And today the acceptance of my death news has proven this.

When I was thinking all this, the bright dawn knocked out the night, it was cloudy that morning with light rains as if the sky too was crying over my pain. Guria wasn't in hostel. She had gone home with her aunt. But as a part of my habit, I went to the ground and like all day I was sitting lost in that fresh air.

Today because of bad weather people were less, I saw a boy was selling newspaper, I purchased one from him. Newspaper yet again had news about Ishika. A long essay was written, and I don't know today after the news of Ishika's death why media wasn't cursing her as it did around a year ago, rather all kind words were written in that essay.

"The young girl had left the world, because in this world she got all the luxuries, but the thing that was lacking in her life was real love and care, that glamorous life in that small age made her everything for the mass. So her worst moments mingled along with the best one, like that it was all caught by the media and was gossiped among the mass.

It was also said she was always appreciated in the news and then cursed in the society and so she had nervous break down which took her life unfortunately somewhere.

So her death wasn't just a secret suicide rather it was a silent murder by the society, and the writer of the essay was giving lesson that the young kids should be dealt with love."

Reading that I was weeping inside in pain but in that rain my tears were invisible, and I thought what a brilliant stunt by media to increase its sale over being so polite ; when I am already dead to them, if they would have shown this same politeness a year ago then may be my life, my identity wouldn't have changed like this. Thinking about it all, may be I was still not happy being Ashika or some where I was missing Ishika. To be honest we all want a luxurious and easy life.

I was so lost in my painful thought that I didn't

notice when a group of street boys came and surrounded me and started singing item song of my mom.

I was scared to see them, but that tall guy whose attendance was also regular like me in that ground, came again like an angel. And made those juveniles to go away. And asked me what I was doing alone in the rain. These guys could have raped me, because they all know it well , that our paralyzed system will punish them after a long run of trials , only for 3years and the jail where they will be sent. There they would get to enjoy all luxuries. Hearing his harsh words I was quiet and was still sitting like a statue, so he jerked my hands and told me that it was raining heavily and I should go, everyone in my home must be waiting for me."

At this in anger I shouted on him, "it's non of your business. I have no home, to my family I am dead on my birthday." My words were may be like a painful puzzle for him, so he was quiet and was looked at me silently.

After a pause he asked me again to go, at this I stood up, but I was thinking where to go? School was closed and in that big and abandoned hostel I was scared to live, then again he said me to move to my way, and I said all my ways were lost.

After saying this I ran towards the railway tracks to die, I was confused and in pain after losing my identity, after being declared dead when I was alive I was senseless like an insane .

So after seeing those tracks I was attracted towards them. He too ran behind me and held my hands. I was shouting badly at him but to calm me, he hugged me tight.

I wasn't understanding and may be I felt some relief with that hug so I too hugged him tight, because since after granny no one had hugged me to support so well during my worst time. I really needed a support of hug to hold me. But then after some time when I was quiet, he wiped my tears and took me to his house.

I had no option so I went with him, but this time I had no trust on any boy. After being betrayed so badly by Vicky, may be all my trust was evaporated from me completely.

His house had two rooms. In one there was a bed, a table and in other there was a mat, some utensils and an old almirah.

In all those rooms there were pictures of a lady and of him, moving to the other room he gave me a towel and his dress and asked me to change before I fall ill due to my wet clothes.

So I did as per he said, then I came out and I found a cup of tea and biscuits on the table, I took it in my hands and was looking over it because I was hardly interested in eating anything. Then he came from other room and asked me to have it before the tea turns cold.

We both were quiet and then he broke the silence and said “In the picture frame, the lady is my mom, who died when I was in school”. I said sorry over this, then he continued that his mom was divorced soon after her marriage because his dad fell in love for some other girl and inspite of saying sorry to my mom he blamed that my mom is a crazy lady and so he had to go to an another women. But my mom wasn’t crazy, if she was a crazy lady then after her marriage when she was pregnant with twins she wouldn’t have topped in graduation at BHU.

But the news of her divorce really made her to go physco, and in loneliness being helpless she was unable to bear the comments of this society to bring up her two children.

"Yet in the phase of her madness my mother didn't try to commit suicide so why did you?"

After narrating the painful past of his mother he paused for a minute, and then he told me that I was the first person to whom he had shared this. So that I could get a lesson of encouragement from this.

I thought that he narrated me the story of his mom to ask me that why I did so, but I was still silent.

Then he said that his mom, his twin brother and he, at the age of seven were living with their maternal grand parent at this home, since his mom was the only child of her parents.

He said that his grand father was retired and used to get a small pension and all those five people used to accommodate in this small room; and the other room was on rent so that money for our meal and for our schooling could be arranged.

In this room of mud floor and thatched roof life was really tough yet the two twin kids were happy, in this room they saw roof leaking in rains, feel furnace in summers and was like a refrigerator in winters and in that small room they used to read, sleep, cook etc. Above all they used to handle their mad mother, whose tough time had made her insane. Some times she used to shout, sometimes used to cry and sometime used to laugh. Like this they spent another two years.

A day when they were in school, their grand father was out to purchase things of daily use, their grand mother was busy washing the clothes, then the weak damped roof with fan fell on the head of their mom and she died.

Though she had stopped identifying everyone years back, but they cried a lot over her death, and the man who made her mad, who was the reason of her death was somewhere happy in his world.

Like this the days went on and after two years their grand father died. And in sorrows after few months their old and weak grand mother also died.

Life already had wounded them so much that their tears were dried to flow over their death, but they used to miss them and were in pain of this great loss.

Now both brothers were 15 years had passed matriculation but had no money to study further, from the room rent they were just able to arrange two times meal a day. Both brothers were left alone in this big and cruel world and so at a very young age we learnt to cope up with the extreme hardships of life.

"My twin brother was sharp in studies and wanted to be an IPS officer, and I was a medium student, who was just able to pass with the help of cheating from my brother's papers. So I decided to work and with that money my brother will study. I started working in a hotel during the day and used to study at night school. Like this, days were going nicely. My brother was able to pass 12 with very good marks and was admitted to the old and prestigious Benaras Hindu University for his graduation in economics .

Since the very first day of his graduation his preparation had started for UPSC, and with my work side by side I too passed 12th somehow from the charitable night school. My brother suggested me not to leave studies so I too had taken admission in graduation in literature from a correspondence course means study the easy language from home and just give the exam.

Apart from studies and work we both brothers used to cook, eat, play and laugh together and our life was getting some what normal. Or may be we learnt to smile soon after being sad. But we never know what the next sunrise will bring.

When one day I was working at hotel, few policemen drunk till neck came and had eaten the lunch well, when I went to them to take the plate and asked them to pay for money, they started abusing me over the name of my mom, at this in anger I told them not to speak all that.

At this one of the officer got up and started beating me and said what I would do to them if they will abuse me? At this in anger I took up the knife in my hand from the table near by and said I could murder him.

He was quiet at this, then the young angry blood inside me made me to spit on him, he was humiliated and the common public was laughing on those policemen who were taught a lesson by a young ordinary boy.

That time they went from there, I thought that matter was finished there, but I didn't know that my brother would have to pay for this.

After a few days a blast occurred in our street at Benaras and many died. At that time from that blast spot I was going back to my home from the hotel where I was working. I was really hurt to see the who nnocents died in that blast, but I walked fast because after going home I had to cook food for my brother and me too. There I saw those two police men were standing and staring at me; who came for lunch that day to my restaurant.

On that very day the B.A part one result was declared, so I was cooking special for my topper brother and was hearing news on radio too, that in the blast two died four injured and some terrorist group was behind this.

While I was busy working, a friend of my brother came running to me and said some hours ago police arrested my brother because they saw him near the spot of the blast and have taken him under custody and have accused him that he was involved with the terrorist in the blast.

Hearing this I said there must be some confusion, my brother is a simple boy and yes at that very time of blast, I was coming back from hotel, and since we are identical twin so in confusion police must have arrested him.

At this the guy said yes it must be the reason because since morning my brother was there in the college. At this I ran to the police station bare footed, because I was lost and saw the same group of policemen with whom I had a mess with that day.

Seeing me they were shocked, because to take revenge from me in confusion they had arrested my brother and had given him such a third degree torture to accept that he is involved in the blast, that his body had turned to red and he fainted.

In his support all student union of BHU came there and so police released my brother.

My brother was beaten so badly over his chest, head, legs that he went in coma, and he was unfortunate enough that he couldn't even get to know that he topped the university exam of economics B.A part first.

He wasn't able to come out coma and from there he went far away from this world, this way in confusion of me Asad, Amaan was arrested and beaten and died. But why those policemen doubted me only by being near the blast site? I still don't know. Was it just a revenge or something else? I still don't know...

I buried my brother but was unable to bury the pain and so I too took admission in BHU just to join the student union, so that what had happen with my innocent Amaan won't repeat again with any other innocent.

So its all about me that how I became alone! And then how I became the president of student union and I earn by teaching students.

So now I don't have to face that hotel again to earn where I met those beasts who took my brother away from me. That's how I went on but have never tried to suicide"

Hearing Asad I was looking on him with tears, this time I couldn't manage myself to stay quiet, though I decided I will never scratch up my past before anyone. But today after hearing the past of Asad, which was silently asking me why I tried to do so?

I stood up and gave him the newspaper where it was all about Ishika and said, "Ishika isn't dead" he was quietly looking at me as if asking me how the star Ishika came here.

Then I proceeded and said just a sentence that Ishika is infront of him, hearing this he was looking at me in shock.

Then I explained him how 7months back, Ishika killed herself and reborn as Ashika. But today on the day of my actual birthday seeing the news of my death, I was broken like any thing.

In a new town, the lonely girl struggled a lot, for what actually I have never ever imagined, like to sleep on floor to have food of charity, yet slowly I started liking this world far from that fake world of glamour.

But today when my hostel students have gone to their homes and I was alone and scared there and then the pain of the news of my death had again broken me so much that I thought to die.

At this he held my hands and said I was a brave girl and made me to promise him I would never try of suicide again.

I too promised to his simplicity, the truth in his eyes made me trust him, which I stopped doing after Vicky, and I said him too, to promise me that he will never leave me alone. I don't know why I made him to promise so.?

He smiled and said yes.! He would never leave me. I don't know why I hugged him and he too hugged me tight. As if we both were longing to hug each other since a long.

Like me he was also in pain and loneliness since long so we kept each other in our arms tightly for a long time, until our heart went a bit lighten from the loads of pain, which was draining out today after a long through our tears.

Then he loosened me from his arms, and said he is going for namaz and I too let him to go with a smile, that moment I realized it's love and so he didn't approach me physically in that lonely house, as Vicky did all times.

While going he said if I knew how to make something then I should keep it ready he will be back soon, after being broken and changed I had never imagined I could fall in love for the second time and even more beautifully.

But it's true. That when it's true love, then its

gravity automatically attracts us to fall in it, with all our trust without any language and a silent conversation of eyes is enough to ensure it.

In these seven months I learnt to make Maggie so I made a spicy Maggie for us, and after he came back we had it together.

While eating it with a smile after a long he proposed straight that he felt love for me and if I want we could marry and so next day I put up a new pink suit and he put up a new pathan suit in which he looked smarter than any hero.

He too complimented me that I was damn beautiful, and in the court we were a registered couple then to keep our relation pious we made it in both ways, that of Asad and of Ashika too.

This way we two, without any people, without any gifts and without any dinners, were the new couple. I had already cleaned and decorated the room in the best of mine before leaving for our marriage.

After coming back he gifted me a bouquet of lily. There were white lilies with red rose in between them and that simple gift was the most beautiful gift of my life.

Lilies reminded me of granny and her true love, and today again the real love of Asad welcomed me in his life with same lovely lilies. Today I didn't know why in the purity of that simple and deep love I was feeling the aura of my granny around.

So on the day of my birth when this world was thinking that I was dead, so I was hurt like anything, then on that same day destiny made me to meet the most precious and the loveliest gift of my life and that is my love.

Its true, God examines us to the extent of our thresh hold to cope up with the pain. This way after a long time of darkness, there came shines in our lives too.

We had dinner together which we made together, and when I was cleaning and arranging the things back, he came silently and hugged me from behind, and removed the curls of my hairs from my neck and kissed there softly.

I smiled and turned towards him, he looked in my eyes and came more nearer to me. I was feeling his warm breath on me, and don't know how I closed my eyes and slowly he planted his first kiss on my lips, in which I was lost and I too started kissing him.

Then he lifted me in his arms and made me to sit on the bed, and then he lay on my lap of red coloured saree with golden embroidery, under the shadow of my hair and we both were holding each other's hands and he was kissing my hands softly.

Then he said, I am not his first but yes! his last love for sure and now he loves me like anything. I loved his truthfulness and was looking at him then he said that when he started going to college there he started liking a girl silently and sometimes with his silent eyes he used to give indications of love to that pretty teenager, may be she too started loving him that's why she too used too wait for those silent signals. Which made him happy.

But those young love birds were innocent and shy to express their first love and before they could have expressed it, destiny expressed its cyclone in his life and Asad lost his brother in a trap.

So for few months he got cut off from the world after loosing his brother with whom he arrived to this world and when after few months when he saw his first love he found she was married and was in love with someone else.

He wasn't ever able to know her name even but I was sure his feelings for her were so deep and true so he expressed it to me too.

Hearing this tears filled my eyes because I was sad to hear his pain and other reason of my tears were may be for the first time my life had introduced me to the true love and that too forever.

I held his hands and said I was the luckiest girl of this world because; I was married to that man who was so true and so pure who loved someone in his feelings without saying a single word without even knowing her name so he must be an angel.

If he would give me just a few percentage of his love, my life would go more like a paradise.

At this he was able to smile and assured me that he loves me with all his love, and then it was going heavy on my soul, though he was knowing about my past life because that was more of the mass than mine, yet I decided to let him know about Vicky.

So I confessed him that I was unlucky enough and crazy to waste my precious first love, over the man who never knew its worth and said sorry to him, because I regretted for doing the best thing for the worst man for the first time.

At this he put his fingers on my lips and said that he doesn't have anything to do anything with my past, I loved him and would always love him, meant everything to him.

Then the thing he said to me made me worship him like a god. He woke up from my lap and sat before me and wiped my tears and then my love Asad said that the man who had broken me I still haven't forgotten him, so if he will be there to love me always then he can't imagine how much I would love him.

At this I smiled and kissed him deep and said I don't just love, care, trust and respect him rather I have started worshiping him and he meant all to me.

Hearing this he smiled and kissed on my forehead and said if I wouldn't have told him about my first love then also he would have loved me as if I were the best wife of this world.

But now with this honesty, I told him all about my past. So now he would love me not just as the best wife but also as the best person on this earth.

Hearing this I embedded my face deep in his chest close to his heart and he was kissing my neck and soon we were lost in each other.

Our hearts were beating as one pace, mind was thinking of each other, breaths were spreading scent as one and we were so close to each other that our soul were also united when our body was making love, with true love and only love...

Chapter 7 - A sweet bliss

"_She was innocent. Yet brave , but a bit insane,
either she crawled , ran or fell but on her own lane...
but far from this world her, heart knows it the best,
He was the one, on whom like a carefree she can rest.....
He made her to happily forget, her weakness and strength;
They moulded in each other replica and merged as one for the entire life's length..."

After a long, after my rebirth; I again got a reason to live happily in this new and lovely turns of my life. This time the reason was more beautiful, more real and so was more precious to me. Now I was so happy that I didn't had the time to miss my old lavish yet hollow life.

For the first time I was getting the most precious thing of this planet and that was love,Which was making each day a reason to live with joy. My world just meant to start and end at Asad and the reason of my life was also just meant for him. So each day more and more I was investing in this true love and it was becoming more pious and deeper and so each day I was getting more in return too.

Now I was going to school to teach the children as Mrs. Ashika Asad, these students were with me when there was no one so they all meant a lot to me.

Asad used to drop me till school everyday and in these days I learnt to cook. So I used to wake up early when he used to wake up for his morning namaz so that I could prepare a yummie breakfast and pack up a tasty lunch for him. Really we can learn even to climb Everest for the sake of love, thus cooking was a small job actually.

Like the sweetest husband of this world, my hubby Asad used to co operate with me in cleaning up our house, which was now a decorated lovely and a more lively home. Even the household chores was like a celebration with him. We used to cook and clean together hearing sweet songs and dancing over them.

Still the other room was on rent because a single room was enough for the two body residing as a single soul there. If at one side at school I used to wait for the time, when it would be over and I would get to go to my home, then at other side my grown teens students started teasing me for this, even colleagues of Asad at his student union party and his tuition students started teasing him that food made with the love of his wife is making him chubbier. May be it was love that was making him more cute and chubby because yet I was not such a perfect cook to serve him the best of the yummie delights.

After coming back from school I used to arrange our dresses wash and press them for the next day; prepare some thing nice for dinner and used to do gardening in our small front yard, and in these months I had grown up a huge bunch of lilies.

Though lilies were my favorite since childhood and now it was more precious to me after my marriage when Asad had given me those lilies which were still therein my diary.

In weekends we sometimes went to friend's of Asad or to my students and sometimes to shop for the things of daily use from the near by market.

It was a new experience for me to take vegetables from the local fruits and vegetable market in that crowd, and to stand in queue for the cereals issued by the government.

All those brands of cosmetic products which I had endorsed once were now like a dream for me, because now my budget was lesser than that of my past daily expenses.

Now even my salary was million times smaller than my past weekly scheduled expense. To be honest and not to sound unreal, nothing was happening to me like those of any hindi films where out of simplicity we start to like even the struggles.

Sometime those sweats of queue, those crowds of buses and other discomforts were making me sad when I used to think about my life which I had once, which I tried to change a lot, but when it couldn't be changed, rather it ended up changing me. Actually that was a made up life,meant for the showoff to the mass,Where my each move was caught with attention and was displayed by media to be discussed among the mass.

Where I had all luxuries and comforts, yet I was in discomforts of loneliness, in pain of no love and care. Then after comparing these two sides of my life, I used to think that whatever I had now is the best and used to thank God for giving me Asad and his true love as a reason to live happily.

In front of all those discomforts, just one hug of Asad's with a smile at the start of day was enough and most valuable for me, than anything to start my day with the best of energy. Its truly said, love identifies the pain behind our smile and happiness behind our tears and so Asad too was able to identify them.

Whenever I used to feel uneasy with these discomforts and so in irritation I used to fight with him over the silly matters or used to make burnt dinner then like a best friend he used to make me happy with smile by putting a cross on that day on calendar to show me that in a month how many times I get angry and all these small loving things really used to make me cool in a second.

With his small steps I was able to spread a big smile on my face. But sometime I used to go sad from deep within, like once I saw my mom working in the movies of adult comedies and boldly she used to say that the audience is matured for this and so there is huge demand which is causing the film makers to make such movies. Hence she does such films.

Now my mom who was a low grade actress, wasn't knowing how much those adult comedies corrode the society, she was moving in Mercedes, so she may never able to know how intolerable it is for those girls who move without security guard in local crowded buses.

Seeing my old life people who were still same even after considering their alive daughter as dead, I was broken and bruised from the depth of my soul in pieces. But in those moments silently the gentle hugs and cuddles of Asad used to support me strongly like a pillar of anchorage.

His love was working on me more than any medicine and prayer and now for the first time I wasn't pretending to be happy, I was actually very happy. This way in that pious land of temples in the city of Banaras, in that one roomed small house me Ashika Asad a class teacher of standard 3rd A , a simple house wife who was feeling her self to be the happiest and the luckiest lady of this planet .

Working for my darling husband round the clock, gave me lot of comforts. Now I was happier and more beautiful; may be just with the home made paste of turmeric, sandal and honey for my face and then yogurt, egg, lemon and henna for my hairs; inspite of those branded weekly beauty care. I don't know I was looking more beautiful now or not, but now my beauty was for my true love only and not for this world and so his love along with simple homely care was making me feel more beautiful.

May be his house was small but his heart where only I was there ,was so big, I was tired working round the day but in his arms I was getting all peace which I lost once and his kisses were giving me all the comforts to live life once more for him.

Sometime when his silent eyes used to speak that he was sorry because he was unable to give all comforts of life to me, I used to try my best to make him smile. I used make him happy with my pseudo fights full of love, and used to shout on him saying that my darling I am having a big complaint from you, why you didn't come some years back in my life so that I could have loved you for more time.

This way my life was passing on so nicely and so well with so much of love I didn't even notice and almost a year was going to complete.

One night when we were sleeping in each others arms, at once I felt so restless and scared. When Asad woke up and sat, I too felt the jerk of his movements and got up with him and held his hands and he too held my hands and leaned his head over my heart.

I was feeling his breathe faster he was sweating and I said "Honey , let me bring water for you", but he pulled me back and hugged me tightly and said, "sweet heart, I cant afford to loose you, you are my life. I can't imagine being alive without you. All left me alone now you please don't go anywhere".

I understood that he had dreamt something bad, I too was scared to see him fearful but to support him, I hugged him more tightly and said "Your life is always with you". Saying this I kissed him with all my passion, love and dedication because if I was the only one for him, then he too was the only one for me and so he too kissed me back with that same passion, love and dedication as if we had never before and made love, so much of love, that this love is everything.

Next day he got up before me, had bath, wore his old black shirt that looked unclean and came to me with a bunch of lilies and bed tea with some biscuits and woke me up with a soft kiss on my forehead, and whispered in my ears I love you my sweet heart.

I was awake but pretended to be sleeping. When he was looking at me with so much of love, when he was kissing and cuddling me, I opened my eyes with a smile, and wished him good morning honey.

But for the first time to see him coming with bed tea, had given me the sweetest surprise. My lover read my eyes and said, "Happy marriage anniversary my love and happy birthday too darling".

At this I held his both cheeks in my both the palms looked in his eyes and said thanks sweetheart.

"You are right. Ashika was born when she met you" and then me too wished him happy marriage anniversary. Then I closed my eyes and he blew over my hairs, it made me to open my eyes with a smile, because I wasn't understanding what was that naughty trick?

But really after that I wasn't able to curb my urge to kiss my darling. That moment I knew he was teasing me and so I too teased back on his lips, and when I was over after a few minutes, then he was looking at me with a smile.

It made me shy and so like all times I buried my head deep in his chest, and he was rubbing his hands and his face on my back and on my neck covered with my long and straight hair.

Breaking that romance I looked at him and asked on this special day, why was he wearing this old shirt? So he said that an year back in the rain, a fairy with tears in her eyes made this same shirt wet when in her pain she first time held him in her arms. His sweet reply made me to kiss him again and this day in that small room we had second honeymoon. Each day was more than any honeymoon there, so I never needed to go for it anywhere. Or may be I was knowing that we couldn't afford it. Yet I was enjoying each moment of life at the fullest for the first time.

Now I was loving and caring for myself even more than ever before. It's really true when we are in love then we try to explore more of our beauty and do try to spread a spell of joy all round, just for the sake of pleasing our love.

One day after a week he came with a box of chocolates and kept it in a corner with of me not coming to his union party.

I was quiet at this because I knew I did wrong, but that time I wasn't feeling well enough to go out. And if I had told him that I am not fine then he would have cancelled his meet to come to me.

So I neither went nor did I tell him that I was not fine. In anger he didn't talk to me, I asked him for lunch but he was quiet. I gave him his clothes to change, but in his anger he took out other clothes. I did not know what to do to calm him down.

So when he went to the washroom, near his towel I put that file of the doctor's report and soon when he came out and after seeing that, he lifted me up in his arms and swayed me around. And said, "Darling thanks! Two big news on the same day". That day he got to know that after 9months he will be a dad and then he shared other happiness with me that his party has got major support and this time he was elected as the president and he would be able to fight for state election.

I was so happy because I knew he worked very hard for it round the clock with true dedication. A noble cause to work for betterment of the common people with his entire honesty.

But I was feeling uneasy and so I screamed, "Please darling !!! Put me down". And with all his care he made me lie down on the bed.

And then he told me not to go to school or to work. I just had to rest, because its not just I am pregnant but he too is pregnant. It made me laugh loudly. He said there was nothing to laugh. I was pregnant with the baby and he is pregnant with the responsibilities to care and love me much, more and the most.

Now every time he used to feed me with his hands. Every morning he used to take me for walk holding my hand in that same field where we met for the first time. There I used to meet my students and all used to greet me and used to bless our coming baby.

Our child was not getting attention of the world before birth but was getting most of the love each second to take birth well and then to live well.

If at one side we were guessing the gender of the child and the name, then on the other side we were praying for him. Each day Asad was loving me more for making us a parents. I too was respecting him more for his care and was asking him would our child be a nice person? And all time with his soothing smile and truth in his eyes he used to nod saying yes.

Though he was damn loving and caring for the day I started loving him, but now his care was billion times more, my husband was caring about me more than my mother had ever cared for me.

I was unfortunate, so i never knew what is the real care of a mother is. Now he used to take me to school and bring me back. My students were even grown up to show more care to me.

He used to feed me with his hand, I had never ever imagined that my life would ever become so kind to me, that it would bestow upon me so much of real love and care and like my granny once again.

With this love and care my last trimester had begun. I couldn't even notice all people who were now my friends in that small span of time in the small town of Banaras used to bless me and my baby.

For this I used to thank God that my baby is shielded with prayers before coming to this world and not like that unfortunate sensational Ishika the intra uterine star whose moves inside the womb were caught by media to be discussed among the mass.

It was the day of my baby shower. In our small home's front yard it was celebrated and was organized by the party members and old friends of Asad's who were teasing him about his crushes of teens on the every second girl of the street, but I was knowing him so well , that his life wasn't so kind to him ever. That he could ever have a happy time for enjoying all these crushes.

But my sweet heart was a master to pretend to be the happiest and coolest among his friends and for this he used to express his crush on every second girl. So with the old gossips, dinner and blessings, baby shower ended and all guests were back home happily. With one of his old friend Asad went for a bike ride and while going I just told him to take care. After he went, alone in the home I was missing him a lot that night. After almost an hour after re arranging the things back I called him but he didn't received, I thought he must be driving so I was looking at his picture because I was missing him like mad that time so just dropped a message saying, "missing you so much honey".

And was waiting for his reply but it was almost an hour and there was no reply, then I was a bit panicked that what is so wrong and so called him back; but this time it was switched off.

I was really tensed and so called his friend and even his number was also switched off, I was really so worried. I started praying and thanks to God that soon God heard me, and I got his message "network problem darling we went far, and now on the way back just reaching you in an hour."

With this I was happy and with a relief I lied down on the bed keeping his photo close to my heart. I was almost falling asleep when suddenly I felt someone is holding my hand tightly.

I was scared and woke up shouting and was so nervous. I thought who could hold my hand if Asad was out and he already said that he would take an hour to come. So without knocking who is this?

With all these thoughts the intensity of my shouting raised higher, so he switched on the light and it was him Asad. I was happy like anything to see him and so hugged him tight he too held me I was normal.

Then after coming back in normal state, I separated myself from his arms and with anger I asked what is this? Why he scared me like this? Why he said it would take an hour to come? At this first he smiled, then held my hands and kissed it. May be to get rid of my anger and always his new tricks really worked on me I don't know how?

My anger was a bit reduced, and then he said to me, that I made him the winner when he was testing me.

To hear testing me, winner etc. I looked at him in shock, and he explained that, when he went for a ride, his friend told him that wives have a habit of doubting. At this he denied him and said that I wouldn't ever doubt on him and so to check it first he didn't receive the call, then didn't reply to the message then switched it off, and they were not too far just 5 kilometres away.

After a pause when he told me there is no network, then I replied him with all my love and trust and made him a winner. But the wife of his friend wasn't able to do so. Maybe she had her own reason, I don't know. Then he said he was looking at me from outside, from the window of our home when I was talking to his photo in the loneliness and was sleeping with that picture of him. So he surprised with this horror thrill; in the extreme of his happiness to make him a winner. With my trust he came by the way of window. To hear all this first I laughed, and told him that he was mad. I explained him how girls always need reasons to doubt. But staying with him for a year now, I only felt love between us grow stronger, so how could there be any question of doubt?

All the time I was so close to him, that even the minutest change in him could be recognized by me. But that change was always filled with more of true love. So my trust too went on rising up with his increasing love.

Lost in my eyes, he was listening to me or may be he was waiting for my lips to stopped its movement so that he could kiss me. So soon I gave rest to my lips after those words and smiled. Then our lips were engaged in the second best thing they can do after smiling and that is kissing.

This kiss could have been gone much longer in flood of love, trust and care, but my baby kicked me from inside and I said ouch and with a smile and I unlocked our lips, he was looking on me that why I felt discomfort. As he was soft.

So for the answer I took his hands and kept it on my inflated belly so that he can feel the movement of our baby inside, after feeling that tender, innocent and the sweetest feeling he was smiling with love and kissed my forehead and I leaned on him and we slept.

Like this the date of my delivery arrived. That day I felt what a mother is and why she is the God on earth and why heaven is in her feet?

Because for nine months I felt each and every movements of my baby when he was eating, breathing, hearing and seeing from me, and now he was knocking hard to come to this world, which was an old phenomena for this world, yet new to me.

To bring him here in this world, I struggled with pains and that pain was so much that there were like at a time dozen of the bones of my body were fractured at the same time. If the pain of a single fracture is unbearable so what to say for that pain. Yet I was alive because I was giving birth to my baby. The seed of my and my life Asad's love who finally left my body and came to this world.

And in a second all my pains were changed to relief to hear his sound and to see smile on face of my life, Asad. I was feeling so blessed and happy.

This way in few years, I reborn as Ashika who was then Mrs. Ashika Asad and finally now Mrs. Ashika Asad, mother of Samar Asad. For his each cry, smile, crawl, words, tooth, walk and yes for his feedings and nappy too we both were crazy. Now the love of mine and Asad's was a bit reduced, because parts of it was now reserved for our love Samar, slowly my life rolled so fast that in a wink it made me damn happy .

Now our baby was a year old, and in our small world, small house but with the biggest love we celebrated his birthday.

Me and Asad now were simple and devoted parents, who were happy in sacrificing everything of their life for their child. Each moment of my life I felt myself so complete and so happy. My world for the people around me may be appearing small but I knew how precious it was. It's worth I was knowing so well, because I knew about the hollow worthless life of the big world where inspite of having everything you feel you have nothing.

I was the best wife, the most beautiful lady for my beloved husband and the dearest mother for our baby and I used to feel so complete with all these, that I never tried to earn titles like yummie mummy. For me mother is just a mother, not a candy or a dish to be served yummy to this world.

Infact I have hated such things, because in the midst of these titles the most beautiful title of a mother was lost from the life of my mom, which had made me to undergo many pains.

But my mother couldn't ever see them because to be maintained as a yum mum she was always busy with more important things than her daughter. Like gym, salon, yoga, aerobics, dermatologist, spa etc.

None of us come to this world after learning about relations but we feel and learn it, and so I too learnt to be a mother no matter how bitter my personal experience was; but for my baby I was trying each moment to be the best mom and for my hubby I was devoting my self at my best for being his best better half.

It was all refining me as the person and all thanks to God. It was my small beautiful blissful world hidden and unseen from this big world and I was meant to be alive only for it.

Chapter 8 - Unexpected is the life...

My Life was on its loveliest swing thanks to God, each day was passing on with smile, care and love. Because of my baby I left going to school but my students were still coming for tuitions.

Now our wishes were small for ourselves and like every nice middle class parent we too started wishing, planning and dreaming only for our son. Now we were forgetting and sacrificing all our big and small desires just for the sake of our son's happiness.

One day when Samar was sleeping on Asad's lap, I brought dinner for the two and with my hands I was feeding myself and Asad. With alternate bites in mine and in his mouth, and when it finished he kissed my hands.

I think now, after we were devoted parents these special moments had reduced. But that bond of our love was growing stronger. Maybe because it was based on the strongest foundation of real love for each other.

Then like all times he was able to read my mind and said that soon he would make all our dreams for our baby come true. And he said after the next day the big rally his party; he will get tickets for state election and then a quarter to live too.

But he said he will not take quarter because

he already has a lovely shelter to live which is more precious than any palace for him. Because in this house there were memories of his mom, grand parents and his buddy brother and last but not the least all best and worst moments of life too.

So he will give the quarter to other party worker who doesn't have a even a small shelter to live. And then like all times I fell more love of that amazing man.

Then he decided that in such a big quarter more than one family can live, so this way the problem of roof for the families would be solved. Then he would deny for the excess expense on his securities and royalties etc. That money was of the nation's. Given by the common man as a tax and should be regenerated and should be used for those common man for their development.

At this honesty of his, I kissed his hands and assured him he will surely win the U.P state elections and will surely be proven to be the best leader.

Because it was my trust on God, such a good man like him could only be a good son, a good brother, a good husband and so a good father and of course so a very good leader too.

With this he said that in the coming years when our baby would start going school, he will not give the other room on rent. Rather he will renovate it for his son. At this I leaned my head on that shoulder, which had given me an anchorage of life, a hold of hope and a desire to dream when I was reborn from my own ashes.

In those tough times, I wasn't like all the girls who left their home, their parents even their last name and with their soul mate and adjust with a new family, new people and a new last name.

Every girl goes through this traditional and

transitional phase, which is a blend of joy and some pain. But I selected this unique transition of mine by myself.

But thank God I didn't have to make adjustment in his new world, rather it accepted with open arms and I surrendered myself truly to it. So have achieved this real happiness and satisfaction.

Thinking about all this, in happiness I kissed his shoulder and couldn't control to spread the real curve of smile on my lips, seeing my love Asad sitting and sleeping beside me with our baby in his lap I was the happiest person ever. So I too buried my face on his shoulder and never realized when a sweet sleep hugged me tight in that absolute silence of glad aura with my husband and my baby.

Next day it was a big day for my life Asad, so I woke up early. He did namaz and I did aarti. Now our baby was able to speak maa and papa and with the charm of his spellbinding broken words we had breakfast together with smiles and then I wished him all the best for his big day. And Samar too in his paapaa words wished his dad all the best.

When he was going, I don't know why I held his hands and he turned to me and kissed my forehead and said he would be back soon by the evening bus with victory.

At this I smiled and nodded my head and waved good bye to him and stood on the gate with Samar on my lap smelling those lilies in the front yard and was looking at him.

When his back vanished from my eyesight, Samar started crying in my lap, I ran to the television and switched it on to see his live speech where my love was expressing his honest views with truthfulness in his voice and innocence in his eyes.

Addressing that big crowd from that creamy stage the leader of "Youth India Party", was illuminating in his same black shirt which he considered lucky for him because for the first time I hugged him wearing that, and when he was speaking his awakening short yet soul shaking speech, and all were quiet as if they were lost in those words of his.

"*I Asad, my identity is that I am an Indian. That's it. I am thankful to the youth of India who supported me years back. I lost my innocent brother in an accident of being accused in the blast, when he was in the college.*

Identity of my brother could have been many more than the accused victim may be of an IPS officer; but today he is lucky to rest somewhere away from this world in peace.

May be by that sacrifice God paved a way to awaken this worthless Asad to rise and to do something for the mass, so that the pain through which I jad been, no one else comes across it again.

Today with years of hardship we are fortunate to build a Youth India Party. With a soul aim towards spreading a helping hand. Its each member isn't very blessed to help other, but they all know it so well what being helpless means and so they are committed to help others at their best.

In this party youths are from the entire nation, above the level of states, religion and casts. Our party doesn't believe in reaping profit for ourselves; to live in a quarter or to enjoy the royalty of government on travel, jobs, admission, medical facilities and security .

Which are actually earned from the tax of million of common man , rather we believe to invest it towards the development of the common man, to carve our nation as an educated India, a united India and so a developed and hence a happy India."

With this, the crowd echoed loud with claps, and then he made all to go silent and continued,

"In this party all youths are united, educated and best of all they are free from any unlawful acts of their past, and so if a party where its each member is clean so i don't think any one will try to harm them so, why should I waste so much money on security?

All are educated so all can earn to lead a simple and satisfied life. So why to suck up the revenue of nation for betterment for our own benefits in the name of royalty ?

We believe in making India, an equal India. Where the load of tax and increment of a single rupees on petrol affects the poor on bus, but the elite class on Mercedes have no issues with such increments. So we plan to pass a bill in parliament asking to impose tax accordingly to the earning, so that taxes and increment couldn't be a burden for the common man.

We plan to make an India where holi and eid can be celebrated together. Our soul is for an India where education will not be just a business center or to give a paper on name of degree without quality . In future for these students get depressed by such fake degrees.

Our aim is not the desire to hold the mighty chair as long as possible at any cost, rather we believe to earn that chair with all your acceptance and we are not even scared to die for doing this noble work.

So if you are ready to stand with youth India to make India an educated, united and happy India then

this is the time to do it".

With this he ended his words of power and truthfulness. The sounds of claps were still continuing in the background roaring higher and echoing. Then some politician came on the stage and covered his black shirt with a khadi shawl as a reward.

Then all news channels were discussing and praising him, but avoiding all those appraisals and media he breached the crowd and those attentions of the channels and took a way back.

Because it wasn't that attention and appraisal he needed, what he needed was to rejuvenate the helping hands. Then on news I wasn't able to see him in the crowd, so I thought he must be free.

So I called him and congratulated him as he did everything in his super excellent manner, and he said that soon he would be coming back to his family to share the victory.

So he asked me to wait, and I smiled. Samar too said paapaa to him, which made him smile. I said him take care my love, and all what he said was , "he love me and our baby a lot ."

After talking to him I wasn't feeling like doing anything. I don't know why I was getting so restless. And was just feeling like to see him soon and hug him.

I had many work to do that time like cooking and cleaning etc. But I wasn't feeling like doing all those. I don't know why? I didn't know what this feeling was, but it was something that was happening for the first time. It made me to feel like I was becoming weak and was feeling alone.

I was trying to do things but wasn't able to do and was just looking at the clock and at the door and was waiting for him anxiously to come.

But three hours passed, there was no sign of him. I dialed his number but it was unreachable. Many times his number had been unreachable in the past, but this time I didn't know what made panic so much

I wanted to hug someone and cry but there was no one, even my son was so small and was sleeping in peace. But may be its said that sometimes the bond of the relations is such, that made my small boy awaken from his deep sleep.

He might have noticed his mom wasn't well. He too woke up with a cry. Other wise he always used to wake up playing. I took him in my lap and held him and I didn't know why he was still crying and how my eyes got wet holding him in my lap.

Soon my phone rang and what I heard was the worst news, that Asad's car met with an accident and he was in the ICU at a hospital.

It made me still, for a moment I felt my heart skipped a beat. My baby was in my lap still crying loudly. But the silent me wasn't even hearing his shrill torrent of cries.

But when the drops of tears from his little eyes poured on me and I felt something was flowing over my neck. That brought me back to reality and I believed I was still alive and would have to be alive for that small life of our love in my lap and for my love struggling for his life in the hospital.

I fed my baby and ran to the government hospital where Asad was admitted in the emergency unit, which was far away from the main line of the hospital entrance. There were many people restless and lost like me because like me they too had someone in those silent, clean and most cared area of the hospital.

In one of those silent units, I saw from the glass my love my life, my God on this land, my Asad was sleeping. There were several pipes attached to his body that poured fluid and blood to his body and the wires that were attached to him by which he was being monitored on the screen.

He was breathing by the oxygen mask. My Asad was appearing weak, lonely and broken and I the only thing I could do at that moment was to look at him with my eyes full of tears. At that time, each breath of mine prayed for his recovery.

My baby in my lap was pointing to his dad and was saying paapa, but this time hearing his wonder words his dad wasn't cuddling him with the same love. When I was lost in looking at him, few people of Youth India Party came to me with a police and they told me Asad didn't meet with an accident. The case is under investigation and police is suspecting it to be a case of planned attempt to murder.

I was quiet to hear all this, may be my anger was lost in my sadness because either it was an accident or a murder but the result was that, my love was cursed of it.

Police asked me if Asad ever had any problem with anyone? Did I doubt anyone? It was hard for me to answer him yet I collected my self from the broken and shattered me and managed to reply to him.

My Asad never had any enmity with anyone, rather he was a very sweet and a helping person. My only doubt was Asad went on the public transport and while going, he told me soon he would be back by the evening bus, then how he went inside the car where he had met with this unfortunate accident?

But all the facts, the replies of what, where, how and when were sleeping silently with my Asad. After this, police went but the Youth India Members were still there to console me and my baby.

Soon doctor came out from the ICU and told us that his head injury was deep and his condition was critical and nothing could be said.

Listening to him I slid and sat on the floor and burst out in tears. All his party members were speechless seeing me, my baby too started crying so for him I controlled my tears and went back home to feed him and soon with a full of stomach I made him sleep. It's best being a child where we just have to make an effort to cry and their necessity of food and sleep is fulfilled to make them happy.

But for me sleeping wasn't possible my home was like a barren land without Asad and each corner was reminding me of him. Where we smiled together, where we cried together, where we loved together and where we cared together.

Today all was same and the only thing which was lacking was my love. The fuel of my lamp, and I had no identity without him. Thinking and recalling all these I don't know when I too slept but early morning I woke up, with my baby. Fed him and went to hospital.

Asad was in same condition in that emergency room, covered with white cloth on a white bed inside the white four walls attached to many pipes.

I went to meet the doctors and they told me that he is still critical and don't know when he will be back from his unconsciousness, and then the expense of treatment of such patient is bit more even though it was a government hospital.

It made me more worried but I said to the doctor to not worry about the expense. I would try my best to manage for the expense. After exiting from the doctor's cabin in the long passage of the hospital. I was sitting quietly and was planning, that I would rejoin the school, will manage to earn by tuition classes of dance, music and painting too and will keep the other room on rent.

But the thing that was making me more worried was that now I have to manage all these tasks with my small baby of around a year, but for the sake of keeping my love alive and to bring him back it was the only way appearing to me.

Soon I saw that as his party members were coming to know about their leader, they assured me not to worry for money , as they will try to do everything to save their leader .

But till then they need another leader. Although no one could take his place, they still needed someone to take his place till he wasn't there so that all can work under that one direction.

So they asked me to be the leader, because none could stand at the place of Asad in his absence better than me being his better half.

Hearing them, I was nervous because being the leader meant again being a public figure, again to have to face the media and cameras. Those question, again I would be discussed in the mass and now I never wanted to be on the same ground, which once had shook my existence, my reality and had changed me and my world.

Now my world was simple, filled with real love and so this small world of mine filled with real love was more precious to me than anything. I never wanted to loose any of it at any cost .

So I refused to be the leader, they pleaded a lot so I said I could guide them to the best of my ability, I will love to work for the party of Asad but not as a leader, rather will work just for the sake of affection for the party, which has clean aim and dedicated member.

From that day after, all my days were coming and going like the storm under the pressure of works and too many things to be done.

I wasn't knowing how days were turning to weeks and making a month, apart from school and tuition of few child at my home for music dance and art, I was all time on foot for my baby who was growing up everyday.

One day he started crawling, then other day he spoke a new word and then next to that he had a tooth growing.

There were days when I used to be tired for the day round work of school, tuition, home. Only the smile of my baby and each day something new in him used to make me somewhat lively again.

I was happy too see Samar growing up but each day at the end I was missing Asad, who would have loved to see our baby speaking with his small tooth in his mouth and crawling on his small legs, in my tough time my students, neighbors and party members were helping me a lot to bring up my baby when I was too busy.

If my weekdays were too damn hectic with school and tuition, then on weekends I was working hard for Youth India Party, going to NGOs to know their problems, making files for the social welfare etc.

Like this how many months passed I didn't realize, but each day when I prayed in my temple, then among those God I had hung the photo of my husband, who wasn't less than any God to me in this world.

The man who let me to feel what life actually is with love , the man who mended my broken heart so well as if it was never broken. The man who erased all my pain. The man who invested so much of love in me that I began to worship him.

My prayers would have been incomplete without seeing my God and so each day I went to the hospital, in these days he was out of danger but was still in coma.

To begin my day seeing his face and holding his hand ,I don't know how I used to get some energy to work round the day. Holding his hands and looking at his face, I used to narrate him about my whole day and night and this small one sided conversation of mine with my Asad was not something less than a medicine to me to boost me up.

Without him I was surviving in this big world with courage, just for the sake of our baby and for the sake of our work on the base of hope, that one day everything would be fine.

I was still thanking God because now at least I had hope for Asad to be well soon and dream for my baby. He was the sole desire to be alive, else once I had already seen the worst phase of my life without any hope, dream and desire.

I used to tell Asad how our baby is learning to take his steps, how his party is working hard without him and misses him so much, like this an year was going to end, and like all days I was talking to him without hearing any word from him, without knowing he listening to me or not.

Then it came our marriage anniversary and I was

broken badly with tears that day Because I was missing him so much. Then an old nurse at the hospital told me not to give up and told me love could do miracles and said that she was witnessing that miracle of love now, because the ultra low blood pressure of Asad's had began to rise up to normal.

Hearing her, I was happy. Because her words were like the ray of hope for me in that absolute darkness. Where I had lost all my happiness, yet I thanked God. That I had my child with me as a hope to dream, to be alive else I too would have collapsed a long ago without Asad.

My mornings were starting from dreams of Asad and then I used to go to hospital first to talk to him. My nights were ending with his thoughts, in these around two decades of my life I was a century old.

Because I had seen life from the two acute phases, it was difficult for me to sleep. Sleeping pills were even ineffective sometime, my eyes were too fatigued and its puffy dark circles were depicting it well.

Sleep was far away from my eyes. Each night I used to write my personal experiences, I used to weave my feelings, my thoughts and my emotions in words to bind up it as a book by the name of "poles of life", because I myself had traveled the poles of life.

And that "poles of life" was all about;

"That our life is like a simple harmonic motion, where it has extreme position and mean position, the one at mean position is simple, small but unsatisfied to achieve the pinnacle of satisfaction.

But that at the extreme position is at its height of best, with all luxury and comfort at the cost of labour, sacrifice, luck, compromise, dedication etc.

We all want that extreme position which requires a lot of energy to reach there, and since the pressure level itself over there is very high, so after reaching there, one again has to work harder to maintain that position there.

So to attain that zenith, all work and work and work, run like the one in a marathon, they do all good and bad. Speak all truth and lies, and ignore whatever little comforts and satisfaction they have in their life to reach that height.

At the end they feel like they ended up attaining those luxurious comfort, but realize that they never lived for themselves? With real satisfaction, pure love and true care...

Rather to get more they loose whatever little and real they have, and its all about the life of a man that starts with simplicity transform to complexity and then ends up after covering the journey of 'poles of life'"

This way I completed a small novel named "poles of life" in a year in loneliness.

If Ishika had written any such piece of novel, before its release its success was guaranteed. But for Ashika who used to travel in crowded bus, didn't know what branded items, car with air condition meant. So for me it was really a very big task.

Such a double standard society we exist in. If someone as rich and mighty as Ishika writes even a sentence, it becomes a block buster; but if a middle class simple Ashika pens down a book then also it is worthless.

Yet I searched out publishers and then I visited the bookstore to know about more publishers. I used to check publishers of all the books and note their names, because google wasn't there that time.

It was little embarrassing to stand in book stores for so long, just to explore the publishers from each novel and not purchasing them because of having such a small budget.

Then I posted the sample chapters to those publishers, some denied straight in a couple of weeks, some asked for money for self finance of the work which was like an impossible task for me and some didn't even reply back.

I didn't understand why. May be my name was Ashika Asad now, it wasn't Ishika Gaur Singh or may be my qualifications were not the top universities or may be my picture was simple and small. It wasn't sharp and classy as once I used to have from the best photographers.

I don't know the exact reason, or may a fact which I didn't want to accept was that my work wasn't good enough for them. So after completing and sending it to various publishers, I forget about it and was busy again in the day round work of my home, baby, my love at hospital, school, Youth India Party work and last but not the least, small conversations with myself in my diary at night when I was lonely and missing Asad badly had no one to talk to, wanted to sleep but sleep was far away from me.

With this, days kept passing. I was busy with all work. And those loads of work pressure actually had helped my wounds to cover, yet it wasn't healed in these months completely.

At Benaras from a just Ashika I became a teacher, a wife, a mother, my baby was growing fast and my students too.

Few of my students were selected for classical

dance competition, and I was happy and excited to hear that my sweet little girls whom I taught those classical movements, were going to perform for the annual program of school in front of big peoples of the city.

But the program was in evening and I was very busy with my baby and all other things, so it wasn't possible for me to attend that cultural program.

I just blessed my small students to perform their best and left for home giving encouragement to them and said, " Next day I would love to see their photos in the newspaper city column and wanted to hear appraisal for them from all the chief guests."

After coming back from school I fed my baby and was putting him to sleep. After that I did some paper work of the party and the associated NGOs.

Suddenly I heard the phone ring. After Asad's accident, I was somehow scared of phones ringing. I was scared of phone ring and today again, I felt the same fear, still I managed to received it.

It's true, some time the unknown fear of our heart is true, which mind cannot understand and what I heard was enough to give a blow to me.

Without thinking anything, I took my baby and went to the school. I got to know that my young student Guria, whom I used to take for walks, that small girl who had now reached 4th standard, was assaulted in the campus.

My mind wasn't able to imagine how the cruel beast could be so crazy with that small girl? Guria was my most beloved student my heart was paining to hear what had happened to her and thinking all these and taking fast steps in the late daytime, I reached the school where there was police and media.

But in the concern of Guria, being her dearest teacher, I ignored even the media, which scared me so much now. I managed to enter the school to meet my small girl in the staff room. Small and sweet Guria wrapped in a white shawl was sitting quietly with the teachers and other girls.

She was silent, tears were there in her eyes, her sweet face was bruised and her hair was messed up. Suddenly she saw me and hugged me, she was crying but had nothing to say and only thing I could do for her was to hug her tight.

I too had nothing to say. After that I calmed that innocent who didn't even know that what had happened to her. Yet being a girl she was able to sense that whatever had happened was very bad and so she was shy and nervous.

Around the police and media, the doctors confirmed it to be a case of molestation.

When all went out , I managed to ask her who? And what she stated was shocking.

She told that when she was changing for her dance, the main chief guest entered the room and asked her where the washroom was and she innocently took him to the washroom. There he started his insanity which was worse than an animal, with that small girl.

She shouted but he continued. Suddenly her friend reached there and hit on his head from back with the heavy jewelry box in her hand and helped Guria to escape from there.

Without caring for anything they managed to go to the principal's office to complain. But there they saw that chief guest already sitting there. Before they could have reached and complain to the principal.

He cooked a story that both the girls were stealing jewelry box and when he tried to stopped her so they other hit on his head and ran away.

Hearing his fake stories both the girls were scared so they told to their guardians, who came there with the police and so the media too somehow came there. That so called big man, the politician or the chief guest was arrested and was making the headlines.

Yet that beast was denying his crime. And Guria's statements were recorded and that sweet orphan went home with her mother's sister.

With anger and tears for the miserable plight of women in our society, I returned back to my home and slept after preparing the file of women's problem for our party working for an NGO for women's upliftment.

Protestors has come onto the street to catch the accused in Guria's case and demanded to hand him. But still nothing fruitful was achieved.

In our country if u have might and money then no matter what crime you commit, you have the right to buy the freedom and judgment in your favour. Unfortunately the one who suffers are always the innocent ones and the common mass.

Next morning was Sunday and so after breakfast I reached the NGO instead of school, to discuss the problems. It was durga puja time where Goddess Durga is worshiped for her divine power and so everywhere there were big tents of her, by the various organizations.

What I saw there was again like a big blow to me, that politician accused of Guria's molestation was surrounded by media and was making speech on women's issue and the worst of his speech was that he was blaming women only for the rise in crime against women.

He was blaming the modern dressing style of the women as the cause of the crime against her. Hearing his nonsense I was boiling inside. I was thinking if dressing sense is the cause then why a girl in suits and sarees are also not safe? If the modern girl provokes the men then how come a small kid like Guria and big ladies more than 60 years of age can provoke them?

Thinking all this and then remembering what he had done to Guria, I got so angry that without caring for any media and any important person present there, being just a women I stepped on to the stage and had given a tight slap on his dual dark face masked white with, the myth of evil money and painted it red with imprints of my palm.

The echo and the blow of my slap was enough to make the noisy crowd go silent.

Once again media and the crowd surrounded me. Lost in my silent anger I moved back from that place without answering a single why and whats of media and people around.

I was back to home and with my baby I was sharing my silence, which had many questions embedded deep beneath. That is why a women isn't save in or out of the womb? Why she is worshiped as goddess if she cant even be respected? Why millions is spent in making her idols and pandals during Dusshera if nothing is spent over to ensure her safety? And why the man who undresses and plays with her modesty is free after the crime and that innocent prey gets to hear the worst from this cruel society? And suffers disrespect to live a shy and humiliated life?

When I was sharing moments of silence with

myself, the members of Youth India Party came to me and said the news of my slap to that politician is on air and was live, hearing them I switched on my old onida tv set whose colour quality had turned miserable in these years.

I saw myself after a long time on television but this time with a new face and a new identity, the party members said it would be fruitful for our party if I will explain for this slap before media.

But the fear of camera and the mass was yet so deep rooted inside me, that I denied any explanation to the media and without explaining anything to any member, the reason of my denial I remained silent.

Then one of the member said he would manage it. I thanked his kind gesture. I knew he had lot of respect for Asad so he respected my decision too without putting any question.

I told all the members that I am not at all sorry to slap that man. Yes! It's bad to hit a person who is elder than us, but being a women what I have done to him is totally justified.

After this they all went back taking the files and reports of my work for that NGO. Then I prepared for the long weekdays with school lessons, tuition classes, wardrobe, my baby's meal and nappy, cleanups process of my home etc.

But each second with all these activities, one thing that was constant inside me that, each second my heart was missing my love, my life, my god, my Asad so madly! So truly and so deeply that nothing in life was appearing good to hold me back with happiness and satisfaction .

But it is true, some hopes and dreams inside us, helps us keep going and so with the hope that Asad will be back, I was alive and with a dream for my baby I was working. Else who could have known better than me about life without hopes and dreams?

I had already seen a life more cursed than this, without any hope, aim, desire and dream and was even poisoned with criticism.

I never wanted any fame now, but my silent slap over the dirt on the name of humanity has made me Mrs. Ashika Asad a school teacher from Benaras, a famous face round the nation.

The mass was supporting me for this in majority. Yet everything, no matter how nice, always have some criticizers too. And may be this fame of mine had reached to those publishers too and so they decided to publish my novel the, "poles of life".

It was a pleasant news for me to hear, yet not so great to made me happy and so in a couple of months my novel was in the market and people were reading and liking it like anything, "poles of life" and it was in the list of national best seller few big producers and directors wanted to make a movie on this.

I had given the huge amount of its earning to the NGO working for the upliftment of women, because my novel didn't mean to bring money and fame for me, I just had wrote my life in that to support the struggling common mass.

All the leading news papers and news channels wanted to interview me, but because of my extreme fear I denied them all in a series. My heart was still scared of the fame and this time my simple and plain denial was in news that Mrs. Ashika Asad a school teacher from Benaras. A worker of Youth India Party a worker for the NGO turned to a successful writer is denying all her interviews for which a common person dreams of.

So the world wanted to know why about this denial? But I didn't have any reply for this. Rather I was hooked in my world with silence and understood that life is always unpredictable.

When you chase fame and wealth, they move farther away from you and when you just work simply in your own world with dedication, without any big dream then unexpectedly they knock on your door and dawns on your ways.

With this yet another year passed. My Asad was still in this world near to us, but away from all. Our baby turned two and half and that sweet boy started going to school.

Its a dream for every parent to see their child going to school wearing a sweet school dress, small school shoes, a funky school bag having brown covered books and note books of alphabets, a colourful pencil box filled with stationary and a lunch box with his favourite food.

Yet, I was unfortunate enough, to see that dream turn to reality alone without my Asad. First day before school Samar went to hospital to take his dad's blessing, to my small boy dad just meant silent Asad on hospital bed sleeping in silence, because Samar must have forgetten those lovely time when he used to play on the lap of his dad and speaking paaapa...

It was weekend I was telling a story to my boy after making him complete his homework. Suddenly the phone rang and this time too it made me scared.

I received it but sometime life feels sympathy on us, when it feels that the chronic pain is above the threshold level of our tolerance. So this time too it had happened to me and the doctor from the hospital where Asad was admitted said it's a happy news for me, Asad is giving good signs and is back in senses and out of coma.

After this news of happiness, I wanted to smile but deep inside me a darkness of fear had made its shelter, which didn't let me to smile, because I was always scared that in my life nothing can go smooth and perfect to give me peace to be happily satisfied.

Hearing this news, was like giving a life to my dead heart and sick mind and in happiness I ran with my baby to the hospital.

Chapter 9 - Life was back again...

Soon after reaching the hospital in an auto, I think I ran like a runner without wasting a second to see my Asad, and as I reached on the door I saw him lying on that white bed with his open eyes and was being examined by the doctors and was surrounded by his friends.

I can't explain seeing him so how happy I was. The smile on my lips and crazy tears in my eyes were small to narrate the extreme level of my happiness that was inside me.

Seeing me with our baby in my lap Asad smiled and at once. Samar jumped off from my lap and ran to Asad and hugged him tightly saying papa.

We all were so happy doctor and nurses told Asad ,that it was all like a miracle and sometime true love and prayers make these miracles possible, else in these years they all had given up, except his wife."

At this Asad smiled looking at me and nodded yes and he said that in that long span of sleep, he used to dream or think, he doesn't know, but inside him he always had a thought about Ashika and our baby. Sometime in that dark world he used to feel that he is in his old world, talking with his beloved wife and those moments were so frequent but very small.

Hearing him tears filled my eyes, and I thought that maybe he used to feel some lively moments in his dark world every time when I used to go and meet him.

I was feeling sad that why I couldn't managed to give more such moments to him. Thinking this I was lost looking at him with my wet eyes and so I couldn't noticed that when doctors left the room and the party men too went out with my son offering him chocolates.

Then I went close to my Asad, and sat on his bed and touched his face. In these days his face had turned pale and weaker and he put his hand over my hands, which were there on his cheeks and to wipe my tears he blew air on my face as he used to all times while teasing me.

With my heavy voice I said told him that he made me wait a lot. While going he had said that he would be back soon with victory but had taken years.

At this he hugged me and said it's the victory of their love, soon I too hugged him as tight as I could have hugged him in my life ever, so that I could never let him go and then he too hugged me the same way. And after feeling his warmth I was alive again and I buried my face deep in his chest, as i always did. To feel supported and secured near to his heart and hearing his each heartbeat and sensing his breath over me.

I was like again in the lively world of happiness, it was hard for me to control my emotions and with my each breath I was saying him I love him so much, I missed him a lot and couldn't live without him .

At this he separated me from him and look in my eyes and said he too loved me a lot, and it is love which has brought him back from the miles. After saying this he kept looking at me and when in the charm of his eyes, I closed my eyes and he kissed me after a long time the same way, and I too kissed him after years to feel that I am still alive. Then asked him get back home my love.

So after more than two years Asad was back to his house. I kept everything in same the way he had left. The only thing I used to do each day was to clean everything, and used to place them back in the same way.

The only change he was seeing in these years, was that his baby was grown up and was going to school.

It was more than any festival at our home, I cooked his favorite dishes like gobi parathas and gajar halwa and then we played with our baby and soon in the new joy of playing with his dad Samar slept earlier. Then after a long, we talked for an hour he was resting on my lap and I was leaning over him and then told him about everything from my school, tuition, party and NGO work to the slap scene and my novel.

At this he held my hands and said he was lucky to have such a courageous women in his life, and after long hours of talks we slept together cuddling each other, feeling each other warmth and touch.

Not just Asad was brought in my life but with him all my happiness and a reason to live, a reason to smile with satisfaction was added.

I was again interested in everything, again all the same things were appearing so beautiful to me, which had gone meaningless to me.

My neighbors who helped me in my tough time to reduce my pain, were there with me to share and increase the happiness too.

Now our works towards home and baby were

again shared with each other. Asad was completely dedicated towards his party work, and I towards my school girls. And both together worked for the NGO.

If I used to cook, Asad used to clean. If I used to teach our baby then Asad used to play with him and vice versa.

Together we were completing each other as the garment to the soul of one other like this, years were going so well.

A million thanks to God I wanted to say that our baby was a very nice and a sincere student. Asad used to encourage him to become an IPS officer for the sake of our nation for the sake of his brother's dream which couldn't be turned to reality ever because of the evils of this society.

But neither me nor Asad put forced him to do anything, he was free to choose the field of his interest. Asad just used to encourage him to be an IPS officer but he had options to him, in these years we started growing old together and our baby was grown to a teenage boy with a soft line of beard and mustache on his fair and long face resembling a blend of me and Asad's with some hoarseness in his voice.

Yet he was a kid for us. In these years Asad's youth india party again rose up with his dedications , my novel was in fame and was translated in other languages too .

Girls of my school were grown up and some had passed from school and some of them were going to college, even the girls from NGO were doing well in their life. Some were working, other were studying further and now our other room wasn't on rent rather it was renovated for Samar.

But even after a decade police couldn't traced who

was behind Asad's accident. Nor could they trace if it really was an accident or an attempt to murder.

Because Asad said the politician who asked him to come in his car, said that he would drop him near the bus stop. Then he went out of the car mid way, saying that he has some important work.

After that what Asad remembered was only, that the driver opened the gate of the moving car and was about to jump out saying, the brakes had failed and after that, the car was hit by something and after that Asad didn't remember anything.

Because after that accident, Asad was able to open his eyes after more than two years, yet police was in lack of evidence or may be the evidences were purchased by the police I don't know. And may be the unsolved case was now closed under those dusted piles of files in each police station of our nation.

Since our life was on track so well by the grace of God, we didn't try to scrap out that painful incident.

Time flew like this with wings, and now we were grown to a mid aged parents and our son was in his 10th grade. Our hard working and sincere son has topped in his tenth standard.

So we celebrated that big day out in the restaurant, I think after one and a half decade I was in a five star hotel. But this time this celebration wasn't hollow the way it had been before. Rather it was filled with real love and so I was more than just being happy .

After a long time I dressed well, yet my sweet Asad used to complement me each day, but today he looked at me for a longer time and complemented me the way he used to a decade back, it really made me feel like no matter we are growing older but our love is growing deeper with each day.

Then we had a yummy delight, and the moment we were about to leave that place; I saw media crowd coming to me, and still I was scared of it and so I tried to move away from it.

But Asad held my hands and looked in my eyes, and in a silent conversation he asked me to face the fear rather than to avoid it .

I too accepted what Asad said, because I never wanted my son to see my fears.

Soon a young journalist approached me and said, "A movie is made on your novel 'poles of life' and it's a big hit and nation wants to hear from the one who wrote this beautiful story and why are you avoiding media? For which every second person strives hard?"

At this I was just able to say, "*I am thankful to the nation for loving my work, I write because I love doing this . It gives me peace and so writing isn't just a passion for me rather it is something very sacred for me.*

I really feel that a good reader is equally important, as a good writer who are able to explore the depth of each word. I am thankful to all those who liked my thoughts.

I was avoiding media because, I am a very simple person and very happy in my small world, I don't want to be discussed in the mass round the globe rather i just want to discover the small and real moments of happiness in my tiny and real world.

That's why I was avoiding media, and then I witnessed a crude fact of life, that when good time comes, it comes with a lot of happiness and makes us habituated of it.

But we never know how and when it slips off and when it goes, we are left so sad that the pain of that sadness is million times more than the happiness of those good times.

Then that toxic pain when it starts to corrode sand destroys us slowly and internally and slowly we are left with nothing and so to avoid that "nothing" I was avoiding interaction with the mass."

My long sentences were may be enough to answer all the questions of media and so with a smile they went.

To win over my fear, I was so happy and looked at Asad who encouraged me to win over it, and with a silent thanks we all got back to our house.

After coming back, Samar switched on the TV like all excited kids, to see his mom's interview on the new channel and finally he was so happy to see me.

After that he went to his room and then I saw on TV that it was interview of Ratika Gaur Singh, my mom whom I was seeing after a long time. She still looked like a hot lady in the age of a granny, with her hi class maintenance regime and me as a struggling middle class lady, hence we both looked of the same age.

See the co incidence, she was now the producer of the movie "poles of life", so I never met her and all money I asked them to give to our NGO for female upliftment, because i never wanted to face my old world again.

She was sitting with Vicky the music director in that movie, seeing her with him I don't know why but I felt pain. Because I have never expected to see my mom with the man who had broken me at the worst. Because of them my life had stopped and then it was transformed completely, yet for them all were still so well and same.

Now my mom, I mean the lady whom I had always seen as the superstar Mrs. Ratika Gaur Singh was playing a few matured roles of a typical mothers. But yes, to act as the best mother, my so called mom was really one of the Best.

Seeing my sad face Asad switched off the TV and said he is feeling tired and want me to give him an oil massage in his head.

I knew it that, Asad had silently got my sadness like all time, and so to make me feel better it he put his head on my lap and I was massaging his head, and he was smiling looking at me and I was feeling so happy to make him feel well .

This way my love has added so much beauty to my life that all those painful and ugly scratches were erased, and then after that oil massage when he slept in comfort on my lap I without realizing, leaned towards the wall and slept.

With smile, happiness and satisfaction days passed so well that now our son was in twelfth and all the time he was too dipped in his board preparations. He himself selected to go for graduation and then to go for UPSC preparation. Asad was so happy to hear that his son will make the dream of his brother to come true.

Sometime we used to tease our boy and asked him whom he love more mom or dad. And all he could reply was, that he loves both of us equally. Then again we used to tease and ask no fingers are equal so how come his distribution of love is equal?

At this he was speechless and irritated over our childish attitude and then used to whisper in my ears that he loves me more than dad but not to tell him, and the same thing in his dad's ears but not to tell me. At this cute attitude of his we used to love him more and used to enjoy his innocence.

Sometime when Samar wasn't around us, I always used to ask Asad with worries that in this materialistic world where a good people are so less and so hard to find, would we be able to make our son a good person?

At this Asad like all times used to hold my hands and used to ensure me that, we are investing goodness in our son so that tomorrow he can make his future bright and things around him well. So we have to be sure that he will be a nice man because we are not building empires for him to enjoy comforts rather we are building his good character to earn respect. At this all I could do was to hug my love my, God, my life my Asad with all my love.

Soon arrived Samar's twelfth board. He was very much dipped in the preparation to give the best of his best, and for his each paper I used to take him to the center which was near to my school and used to bless him.

Now his just one paper was left, we were only able to talk to our son for small time during the time of dinner else he was always busy with his studies. We planned that after his last paper we will go for a picnic together.

On the day of his last paper I had a speech at the NGO and so my intelligent son, who was now a grown up boy to reduce my worries he told us while we were having dinner a day before his exam that with his mom he started going to school so with his dad he will end his school.

At this Asad looked at him and said him, "sure my champion" and kissed on his head, and I was looking at the treasures of my life, my son and my hubby with love and with this I too went near them and put my arms around both of them and said we are proud of our son.

We all shared a happy and a precious smile together then Samar went to his room to study, I kept the things back in the kitchen and cleaned the bed, Asad lied on it like the all days. Then I brought a cup of milk for Asad and Samar and instructed them to brush after that.

Then after cleaning the kitchen, preparing mine, Asad's and Samar's dresses for the next day and after making a small preparation for the next day's breakfast, I opened my hairs to comb them, and don't know when Asad came and hugged me from behind with a naughty gaze.

Then he said "Our son is growing up, but his mom is still so young and beautiful how is it possible?". I could see him from the mirror. I held his hands which were on my waist, and said, "Its all because his dad loves me so much".

At this he lifted me in his arms like a newly wed bride and took me on to the bed and loved.

Next morning I fed Samar his favourite parathas with my own hands because he was revising his chapters for the last exam and to Asad too because he burnt his hands while ironing his shirt.

Then I hugged and blessed Samar for his paper and said bye to them and went inside, then Asad again came in and said that he had forgot something. And when I asked what? He hugged me and said "this".

At this I smiled and kissed him and asked him to go fast, and then I cooked lunch and packed it and left a note on the table for Asad, "bring all the food, mat, music set and game set for the picnic. I will join you both on the spot after my speech at NGO".

I don't know why today I wrote in my diary in the morning on the 15th march 2013 that "I feel like I am the luckiest and the happiest person on this earth and I have no complains from my life, then I took a few of those dried lilies in my hands and kissed them, they were those lilies which Asad had gifted me on the day of our wedding and since then till now he made my life lovelier than those lilies with his love"

At the end I penned down a poetry deep from my heart.

"I didn't reveal, when I was in the state of pain,

Because I knew u had no cure, except the advices of no gain...

If I had explained, you would had looked me down as miserable,

And I couldn't have ever achieved of what I am really! Able....

But when I rose from my hardships, I did announce,

So that "you" will follow me as an inspiration renowned....

I actually wish sometime my son gets to know this and feels about the depth of life and grows as the best version of himself.

Then I locked my home and looked over it once andgave the keys to my neighbor and went to the NGO.

The moment I reached the NGO I saw on the gate that man whom I had slapped a decade back was staring on me. I felt uneasy about that but ignoring him I moved in and went on the stage and began my speech on the evening of women's week.

"All women are special, and so I request all the women recognize your value. Search your happiness from you and never expect it from anyone other than yourself.

Because it will disappoint and break your tender heart.

If something went wrong don't regret it because flaws and downs are the part of our life, rather take lessons and move on for the ones who really care for you.

World is so opportunistic. Never let it exploit your innocence, don't regret for your mistakes because we all human do commit mistakes. Whatever good things you did out of your innocence for the bad people just let it go.

What ever I spoke before you, all were my self experiences and thoughts. I want to put forward some question to the society .

That if a girl has to marry then why don't people ask about her academic, merit as if beauty and house hold works are the only criteria for her and her only worth.

But for the boy they proudly tell about his merits and academic performance no matter how he is in all other things, if the girl works hard in her studies from school to college to build her career for the sake of her parents and her family then why her identity according to her in laws is still restricted in the kitchen?

And, unfortunately her respect is measured on the amount of gold she brings as dowry, why she can't care for her parents after her marriage, but a boy can?"

Soon after ending my speech I was about to leave the stage, I was in hurry to join my love and my baby for the picnic, but don't know why and when a bullet hit me?

It made me feel like I had to leave this stage of this world. The audience sitting soon turned into a running crowd in my hazy view.

In my last thoughts, in my sinking pulse, collapsing heart beat and diminishing views, what I remembered was the face of my son and my Asad in our small home in a series of sliding memories, right from the day I met Asad and with him how life knocked on to me again with love, care, happiness and all satisfaction.

I was remembering only this in those moments in my state of pain.

Chapter 10 - This day...

I Samar Asad, after completing my last paper of twelfth board came out of the gate with the feeling of excitement. Because I remembered the promise which mom made to me that after my paper we would go for a picnic together.

On gate among the crowd, I was able to see dad in his old and favourite black shirt. My tall and fair dad was standing out in the crowd and so it was much easier for me to identify him.

Seeing him in excitement I ran to him like a proud kid to end his papers so well. But seeing my father anxious, nervous and tensed from a few steps behind. I couldn't sense that something has gone wrong beyond the level of my expectation.

After going to him what I heard from his heavy voice made me still in pain. I was shattered to hear that mom was attacked during her speech at the stage, a bullet had hit her body and she was unconscious and so after an hour we would have take her to Delhi by air for her best treatment.

Hearing dad on the way to hospital, I had a series of questions in my mind to ask him how it happened? When and where etc. But neither I could ask nor dad could explain it.

The news of our pain was the news of the nation, may be people were discussing about it. I don't know what gain anyone could get in targeting my angel like mom. Who never had even thought of harming anyone in her life ever. Yet she was rewarded with the worst.

With all these thoughts we, the small people of small town reached the capitals of big people in just less than an hour. Our national capital New Delhi was cleaner, greener and faster than my place. Yet it was stranger to me, and my mom was admitted in the hospital in room no. 7 in ICU.

Dad was lost in his silence and I was lost in my sadness. We were so broken without our mom, that we were even unable to support each other. We were hungry, tired, sad, silent and broken. But we just had one feeling at that moment and that was pain for the condition of my mom. We had no word to explain this to the media and to the police.

In our hearts there was an unknown fear, which our minds could sense but we still prayed for speedy recovery of her. May be the condition of my mom was very critical so even the doctors were preferring to stay silent.

I didn't notice how twenty four hours passed and the evening of sixteenth march came. I just remember that on fifteenth march evening our ambulance had reached to that hospital. In my mind the last words of my mom were echoing, her blessings which she had bestowed on me a few days back and her promise that we would go for a picnic together.

But all of a sudden all those granted words had changed to everlasting memories, because my mom was struggling for her life.

In news the condition of my mom was being telecast. The on her had brought a clash of groups at my hometown Benaras.

I was least interested to find who were those groups, their reason of clashes etc. The only thing I was wishing for from the bottom of my heart was that someone somehow brings my mom back to me.

On sixteenth march evening my mom was back in the senses, we were happy to see her. My brave mom in her pain might have sensed that clashes would happen over her attack. So for the first time she invited media to say, “no clashes, it will affect the innocents.”.

After this she wanted to say something to me, I was holding her one hand and dad was holding her other, but we all three had two things in common, and that was our silence and our wet eyes.

At this my mom with her breaking breathes managed to say dad, “I will always be around you and so you have to take care of yourself”, then she looked at me and smiled then opened her lips to speak but her pain didn’t gave her any chance.

She was trying to keep her eyes open and fixed on me yet they were weak and were going paler. She was continuously pointing towards the ‘mirror’ , as if she was trying to tell me something.

But she couldn’t, her last time couldn’t grant her any extra moment to reveal the depth of her heart. I felt her hands in my fist turn cold, her eyes were fixed on me like a stone.

And this way when the roosting birds were quiet in thy nests and the darks of night covered the dim rays of saffron evening, that very moment angel of death came and took the pure soul of my mom’s far away from us and from this impure world.

This way my mom left dad and me alone. The

best hospital and the best doctors of big capital couldn't bring her back. May be her last breath has pulled her to the soil of Delhi.

We took her back to our home soil Benaras and there she was burnt and her pious ashes were submerged in holy ganges and a few were buried in the courtyard of our home because she always wanted to live in that house. There, dad planted a lily plant.

From all the corners of my small home I explored all the mirrors and finally from one mirror near to the picture of God, I was able to get the complete reflection of my mom's life.

So that day I began reading about my mom who came to this world as Ishika Gaur Singh with all celebrations and hollow promises and left this world with sweet memories and solid values but far from the view of this world.

In a day I read that diary of my mom, from which I came to know how this tough life had made her travel a long way from one pole to other.

In this journey she was transformed from one scintillating contrast of Ishika to the other paler contrast of Ashika.

After knowing her past, her struggles, her bravery, her sacrifices the level of respect in my views had raised much and more higher.

Now I wasn't respecting her just as my mom, rather I felt like saluting her as the best women on this earth, who devoted her best in the each harsh and soft moments her of life.

After going through it, I felt why my mom indicated me towards the mirror in that last stage, so that I can have a look over this precious journey of her transformation towards simplicity.

Now in a day after reading it, I got to know many things about this life. That it is full of obstacles, there is no perfect time to start anything, rather we have to make the perfect move with these obstacles.

The real beauty of this life lies in the small things and discovering its happiness in them, not in the search of bigger happiness at the cost of sacrificing smaller ones. Otherwise today we all wiould be unsatisfied in search of satisfaction

The moment I completed reading the journey of my mom from the "poles of life", I felt that the dusky dawn was illuminating the curtain giving a knock that soon sunshine will be spreading around.

I closed that precious diary and kept in behind the frame of God in which there was reflection of my dad pic, and ran to the court yard of my home, towards that lily plant .

Then after thinking about something, I went out of my home and plucked a few white fresh lilies from the common public garden and its buds and stick them on our lily plant in our courtyard.

Then I spread perfume of lily in the courtyard, so that when dad wakes up, he would be happy to see that mom and her memories are around us. That is why this plant is bearing the flowers so early in a day, because mom's ashes are present in its roots.

So to show it to my dad, I went to dad and woke him up to come out for a fresh morning walk.

Dad came out, after waking up like all days habit, his eyes were still searching for mom and were missing her, then dad came out and he was sensing the lovely fragrance of lilies.

I said him, “see dad mom is so near to us that’s why this plant is having her favourite lilies so early, and so having such a strong scent in abundance.”

At this my dad smiled touched my cheeks and kissed my head and looked on the sky and said, “see Ashika our son has grown up so fast to such a nice man”.

At this I smiled and hugged my dad and said in my heart, that each day I would wake up before dad to put lilies on the plant and to spray its scent.

Four Years Later...

At the hotel LE MERIDIAN in New Delhi the success party for the top 10 UPSC toppers of the nation was held, hosted by the coaching institute where I did my preparations for All India Civil Services Examination.

In a room of around more than 100 people along with media and some known personalities of the country, I Samar Ashika Asad, was sitting in the first row in my blue suit, with my mid aged yet handsome dad Mr. Asad in his old yet most favourite black shirt and blue pant.

Soon announcement was made on the stage "India's youngest IAS officer, Mr. Samar Ashika Asad , please come on the stage. Who hasn't just topped the UPSC examination, but also set the bench mark of highest score so far.

I was so pleased to hear this, tears filled my eyes out of happiness. To see the pride on the face of my father over the announcement of my success I was overwhelmed.

In my blue suit, the first suit of my life, that my father had gifted me for my success. I think I was looking almost like my father; a young replica of my fair, tall and handsome dad.

With high held collar of confidence I went to the stage and before I could say my prepared speech, tears filled my eyes and made my throat heavy.

So many things were going inside my mind, about my lost mother and my parents struggle to make me an IAS officer, that I forgot my speech in those moment of scrambled emotions.

I controlled my self, so I took the help of a dry smile and went aside and drank a glass of water to calm me down.

People were looking at me with surprise, because they wanted to hear from this record making IAS officer.

Then I began to speak directly from my heart.

I Samar Ashika Asad, first of all want to congratulate all those who cracked this tough UPSC exam, though I topped it because it was my dead mother's dream yet you all deserved to be appreciated.

My identity before being any topper, is that I am just a simple and a true Indian. Today here I don't want to share my feeling or a tale of my struggle, rather want to narrate a small story, so that it will give a boost of encouragement to the millions of struggling youths of our nation.

I hope you all know about, the sensation of the nation around 44 years back Miss Ishika Gaur Singh, who was the most luckiest and the mightiest kid of the nation, but about her its said that she under went the prey of nervous break down and had committed suicide at the young age of 18.

But the fact is , she didn't die. Like a Phoenix she burned herself and rose back from her own ashes as a simple person.

You all must be wondering why I am talking about her now? It is because she was my mother. Whom now this world knows as Late Mrs. Ashika Asad.

Actually that scintillating world had given so much

of luminosity in Ishika's life, that her vision went blurred.

But when she sensed the reality of the void of satisfaction in her life, the ground of existence was shaken.

So she transformed her self to a simple Ashika and to achieve peace; she restarted from a small town as a common mass of Indian crowd.

With the tale of my mother, I don't advertise that we should transform ourself to achieve something in life, but yes what I explored from her journey and from her national best seller novel "POLES OF LIFE" is worth sharing:

I want to give a message, that everyday just do a simple thing, stand before the mirror and question yourself for your each big and small , right and wrong deeds.

Then try to justify yourself, and see if the inner you is satisfied from your replies or not.

If you aren't satisfied with your own answer, if your heart pains with some unjustifying deeds or if you are scared of them, then still its not too late because still Almighty is there some where in your heart. You just need to explore him with all your truthfulness.

And unfortunately, if you are not sorry, for your any wrong deeds and satisfied with your answers, then evil has captured your heart and has made you its slave, to satisfy its desires of all the worldly lavishness, and to achieve those desires you forgot, the fine line of demarcation between right and wrong

What I shared is a simple formula my friends to refine you and to explore yourself. Just try it. At the end you will find it a method of your spiritual revival."

So with this I want to end my tale....

Thanks a lot to this lovely audience to bear with me.

Jai Hind!!!!"

With this I finished my speech and the whole hall echoed with the huge round of applause.

Then I saw my smiling dad, who came and hugged me when I stepped down from the stage .

I was sensing a strong smell of lily that time. I thought some one has put lily perfumes, and then we went out of the hotel after the program had finished.

On the way back to the New Delhi railway station, we crossed a temple and a gurudwara. I bowed my head in respect as it reminded me of my mother.

Then came a mosque again I bowed my head in respect for my father and then came a church which reminded me of my mom's most beloved granny and again I bowed my head in respect.

After some time, my dad asked me, "did I too feel a strong smell of lily in the function hall and then near temple, gurudwara, mosque and church?"

At this I smiled and said, "Yes dad".

We both looked each other with a very happy smile, to sense lily and to feel the presence of my mother around.

So this way her happy spirit came to see the success of her son and then I understood that her pure soul was residing in all the sacred and actual four pillars of our nation.

So actually the four major pillars what Ishika witness is a just a smaller version, rather the actual and magnified base of our great nation is 'The unity in diversity.'

So me, Samar Ashika Asad an IPS officer took a pledge silently deep in my heart, to serve my glorious motherland with all my honesty.

May it rise from the darks of dividing policies of the white collar dirt, and go beyond region, cast, religion, sex, colour and grow as the best nation and regains its lost glory."

So me Samar who didn't believe much in God today had realized that, God is one and so all religion advocates humanity. Thus I felt my angel like mom sacred soul near all the sacred places of worships.

Now everyday I wakeup early and wake up my father for his morning prayer, and light a candle in the prayer room of my mom and put garland of lilies over her photo frame....

So it was all about my mother Ashika Asad and her poles of life; through which you witnessed the shades of our life and faces of thy Nation.

In these spans of years the one who hit my mom was caught but our slow judicial system couldn't punish him yet, may he and all criminals of the nation can be punished soon so that the criminals identify the power of system and victim can trust on the system

" Justice delayed is justice denied" May it can be proved wrong soon.

3 years later-:

I (Samar) married my fellow UPSC friend Asha. We have an year old daughter and we named her Ashika.

She has inherited the genetic face of her grandmother and so she resembles Ishika.

My dad, my wife and our little Ashika and I are a happy family. Our small girl is very attached to her grand father.

When ever our young Ashika cries, we take her near the lily plant of our home and she stops crying and puts on a joyous smile. May be find the fragrance so soothing...

A Few Immortal Lines.......

I, DEATH. A crude fact of life who finally takes everything. So when I was taking Ashika I was seeing in her eyes that there was only one desire that some more time she could have to spend with her love Asad and her son Samar.

But she was so tired that she surrendered herself to me and closed her eyes and easily came with me, with a sense of satisfaction, because she was carrying very good deeds with her to her next world.

Really true. At the end the only asset that we can take with us is our goodness, rest all properties goes waste for us.

Me MEMORIES. When death takes every thing, I am the only one who resides in this world, and so today in this function hall I was seeing a lovely glimpse.

That pretty Ishika and beautiful Ashika sitting in white saree with white lillies in their hands with a pure smile on their faces and some tears in their eyes. They were sitting together holding each other's hands hidden from the sight of this world.

This way death will keep taking lives and memories will try to keep them alive. Under the layers of time this processes will go on and on, but some tales so true, so touching and so inspiring like "POLES OF LIFE", will be alive forever and ever.

I LIFE; the truth and important existence of this Earth,

Every moment and in every lane, I will take birth.

Sometime in some face, I will just make here an entry and will go;

But sometime about some face, you will love to know.

I am like a heaven to some and to other may be I am a challenge great;

It's on you, that you tried to carve me or left it upon your fate.

A lucky past, made history hardly I had witnessed,

But hardships was many times, the cause of brightness.

Death will take me, but memories will try to keep me alive,

So it depends, what deeds here you preserved inside.

WRITTEN BY-:
DR.FARAH HASEEB.

Dear readers,

Hope you enjoyed travelling this journey of her, through the "poles of life"

So if it touched you , then kindly do share your experience and please! Write the feedback to me on.

farahhaseeb5@gmail.com